Arthur Robins

Crispin Ken

Volume 1

Arthur Robins

Crispin Ken
Volume 1

ISBN/EAN: 9783337382414

Printed in Europe, USA, Canada, Australia, Japan

Cover: Foto ©Andreas Hilbeck / pixelio.de

More available books at **www.hansebooks.com**

CRISPIN KEN

BY

THE AUTHOR OF "MIRIAM MAY"

VOL. I.

LONDON

SAUNDERS, OTLEY, & CO., PUBLISHERS

66 BROOK STREET, HANOVER SQUARE, W.

1861

The right of Tranflation is referved

To the Right Honorable

Sir Edward Bulwer-Lytton, Bart., M.P.

This is, by permiſſion, gratefully Dedicated

By

The Author

CONTENTS

OF

THE FIRST VOLUME.

Crispin Ken.

CHAPTER I.

How the Perpetual Curate of St. Hilda's kept Christmas Eve.

"THINK I could eat a bit of something now, Jack; I have half a mind to try," said the perpetual curate of St. Hilda's, in a thin uncertain voice, which might have gathered up more strength had that "bit of something" in its coming not been so long about it.

"Jack is out, father; he went to Mad Meg's an hour or more ago."

"Ah! Crispin, is that you," said the

curate; "sit you down near me—nearer
me, where I can feel you; for it's well to
me to have you by my side again; but in
waking up it strikes so chilly like; we will
have some coal, and Crispin, I am glad we
are awhile alone, for mind you, I have a
thing or two to say to you; and tell me,"
said the curate, looking eagerly into the
face of his son, "is it so long a time that
I have been sleeping here?"

Crispin Ken drew near his father, and
seized the thin damp hand that was
stretched out to him. He, too, for days
and for weeks had had something to say,
but when he felt that hand, that hand so
heavy yet so thin, it was not in him just
then to begin at all, whatever he might
have to tell.

"Crispin, what ails you, boy, that your
hand is never still? I say it's never still;
likely enough though it's the cold; a bit
of fire will stay that chill; there's stick
and coal about."

Crispin Ken did not know how he
should meet this; he would a great way
rather

rather not have met it at all ; but he could see his father's searching eye upon him, and he said, " there was, a week or more back ; the coal is gone, and we owe for the last, and there is no credit for us now."

" Well, well, Crispin, keep up your heart, boy ; God will not see us over hungry ; throw on a stick and strike a light ; and is there a chance bit of anything about that I could eat, think you ?"

" I would rather, father, that you did not ask ; the last bit of wood was used to warm your broth this morning, and we have done without a candle end ever since last week."

" Never fear, boy," said the curate, who had the more need to be holpened himself, " things have got to their worst ; things will mend ; but it is very cold, and I think I could bear my heaviest coat about me."

" Your coat, father—coat—which ?" said Crispin, staving off what seemingly would have to come.

" Oh, I have only one, Crispin," said the perpetual curate, forcing a smile, the

better

better to bear up his boy, " but it is not what it used to be, it hangs up there."

It had hung there for more years than ten, but it hung up there no longer now.

Whilst the sick man slept, and yet seemed so likely to sleep, for his waking there must needs be fire and food. The coat should have been by then a hostage in the pawnbroker's hands, but it had not been taken down till there was nothing left besides. The perpetual curate of St. Hilda's had asked in his waking up for a bit of something he could eat ; he had asked for coal, he had asked for light, and now it was not for him to feel his ragged coat was his.

" Crispin, you have something that you want to tell ; God will strengthen me to face it, but I cannot wait," said the wasting man, in a whisper that showed no strength had come ; " it must be now—now. The worst, Crispin, if it is worse than what I have faced, must be better than what He has for a while chastened me to bear, and that worst, Crispin, I must have you tell."

How

How could he so bidden speak—speak, where the life was such a shadow that it hardly seemed at all a living thing? How could he tell that where hunger had come hunger would stay? How could he tell that as that coat had gone it might be that no other coat would come? and harder than this there was that which Crispin dreaded. The cold sweat broke out, and stood upon him as he thought that any of the season's many signs might tell his father it was Christmas eve. The doctor, who had only to order and not to find, had said, "Give him to eat when he awakes or likely he will die; my drugs cannot fill a belly that is pinched for food; he must not wander; he must not think on what has been. His mind will go back, and where it so goes there it will stay:" and Crispin Ken knew what this might mean.

By the little light that there was he could see his father had relapsed into what was his habitual fitful sleep. If anything, it mattered little what, could yet be got upon the coat, there might be to the

curate,

curate, yet, a waking from that sleep; but he knew better than he could bear to think, how many levies there had been upon that coat. He could nothing hope; he dared not fear.

"It is the last thing that I would come to touch," said Crispin in a whisper to himself, that he meant should justify what he might do; "but I must save him," and as he spoke he crossed the room to where the picture of his mother hung.

The memory of what was dead was very fresh to him, and it is not well if to us that memory is ever like at all to die. It cannot, put it to what test you may, it will not die. I have seen it come between the heir with those wild oats in his hand, and the kiss of hell, the wine cup and the leg; nor yet one grain of those oats there shall take root or straw whilst the memory of a mother lives. For every mother's memory held fast, the circles of the damned shall be the poorer.

That image was the last on which Crispin would have laid his hand; but it was a

print

print of price, and many weeks of bread
were in that picture frame. He had taken
it from the wall, and by the little light of
the moon was feeling for his hat, when he
turned about to meet his father's eye.

"Crispin," said the curate, struggling to
raise himself in bed, "what may you be
doing with that picture? I must see that
there."

"I am going to turn it into money,
to make it into bread; the doctor says
you must be kept up. I am hungry
myself—it is not that, God knows—
but I cannot sit by here and see you
starve."

"I know you would do anything for me,
Crispin, — anything; you always would,"
said the curate, holding out his thin arms,
"and that makes me care a bit the less to
ask you this. Listen to me, Crispin, unless
I have your word, and have it now, that
whilst I live — no, no, that won't be long,
— that whilst you live, that picture never
shall be bartered for money or for bread,
never, but to save our honour, for the

nights

nights and days I yet may live, I will never take my eyes from off it."

The son knelt down and spoke the words, and the perpetual curate of St. Hilda's restless breathing awhile was all that might be heard.

"What's that, Crispin, I heard a hand upon the door?"

"It's nothing, father, nothing," said Crispin, who did not quite mean this, "only the wind which shakes the bar."

"There, boy, there, don't you hear it? there, again?" and this time Crispin knew that he must show his father was not wrong.

"Oh, if you please, Mr. Crispin, it's only summut for the ringers; it's always been a reg'lar thing on this ere eve for twenty years."

The curate's son did not at all know why he should be ashamed when the man, who had only taken one answer for those twenty years, should have gone empty away. It might be it was not so regular that a perpetual curate should want a " bit

of

of something" he could eat on getting round from a long chill, or a bit of fire, or the coat that should have been his very own; but Crispin knew that things not well to hear might very well be said by those who once in twenty years had gone without their shilling.

"Who was that, Crispin?" said the curate; and this was asked with words that hardly could be set aside.

This was what Crispin had dreaded that his father should ask, so he was minded that he would not tell him.

"It was no one," said Crispin, who was awkward over any lie.

"What might no one have wanted at my door?" asked the curate searchingly. "Look you, I know what he wanted," his voice more hard and his manner wilder than of late, "it was the ringer, Crispin, the ringer that I always paid at Christmas time; why does he come now,— now,— when it isn't Christmas time at all?"

The doctor had said he could not answer for it if the perpetual curate of St. Hilda's

came

came to wander, and the perpetual curate now so wandered that he thought that it was spring; but the bells rang out clear, and the curate knew they never chimed like that on any night in spring.

"Those bells are ringing, Crispin, as they do on Christmas eve," and the curate looked wistfully and terribly into his son's face, and that son heard him say, "Is *this* Christmas eve?"

The curate did not ask this as he had, since waking, asked anything before,—it was a searching cry that would take no answer but the truth.

"Father, this *is* Christmas eve!"

"Christmas!—Christmas eve, boy! then I ought to be glad; help me up, Crispin. I must go and see your mother hang the holly in the church; where is she, boy? It seems that she has stayed away so long,—it chilled her once: tell her not to stay."

"Where is she?" and so the dying asked where was the dead.

Crispin held his very breath as he watched his father's face, so tortured by the

the clinging memories of the past, as it witnessed then that father's was.

"I have dreamed dreams, Crispin, of Christmas eve, and of your mother, and of her hanging up the holly in the church; and she kneeled, and doesn't she kneel now, before the altar, as she did when we were joined for ever? But sit you down boy, you are like her, and let me feel you — you are left;" and the crisis, till another one should come, was past.

"I will get up, Crispin, I am stronger than I was—it may be that I shall not keep another Christmas eve."

"You forget the coat, father. Jack can't be so long now; and if he have luck with it he will bring back a bit of coal."

"I could eat a something, too, if it was here," said the curate, looking quite as though he could; and then he continued, "surely Jack is a while returning," as the minutes, which to them seemed weary hours, rolled on.

"He has gone out of his way a step or two to Mad Meg's; there's no one here-

abouts

abouts at all like Meg to get a price in pawn," said Crispin, who, perhaps, was beginning to show he feared that this last journey of the coat might have been at a discount.

"It ought to be good for something, that coat," said the curate, with a show of reliance in an old friend; "of course, it doesn't matter much, or perhaps anything at all, but I suppose it hadn't got my name. I shouldn't like people hereabouts to talk for the sake of the church, Crispin; but where has Mona been these many hours?"

"Mr. Lyle sent down about sunset to say he should be very glad if some one could come up as soon as might be to the Hall; and Jack had to go round to Mad Meg's, and so Mona went to Mr. Lyle's, not but what I think," continued Crispin, "that this summons seemed to her —"

"Do you know," said the curate, looking in the main well pleased at the suspicion, "I am not so sorry Mona went; and I often fancy, Crispin, that I could see *that* happen yet

yet before I die; I think he likes the girl right honestly."

It was not so hard to see what Reuben Ken might mean.

"I have often fancied," continued the curate, half musingly, "that he took to the girl from the first; but what is that to me?" he said, as though it was just everything to him; "likely enough, what's best will be."

"Not if she should ever come to be the wife of Ruy Lyle, father," said Crispin, almost setting his teeth against the thought of such a bargain; "and could she keep her place in your heart if she showed so false to Wycherley?"

The curate gravely pondered his reply.

"Would you have her starve, boy? Hasn't she served her time at that already?"

"Starve!" said Crispin, "we well may all do that; flesh of *his* flesh—God forbid."

"Crispin, since you first talked you were ever bitter, ever seeing what you cared to think was dark; how has this man, Ruy Lyle, drawn out your hate?"

"I

"I do not hate him, father—I have no cause. I have no cause to know that he is either ill or well; but I would not have her love him."

"And how is she so much above the love of a good man?"

"A good man, father? I would that I could look upon his face and think it."

"Can you charge him with a crime to justify this little liking?"

"With none," said Crispin, bitterly. "He goes softly; he gives alms; but did you ever feel at ease in the presence of so very good a man?"

"Crispin," said the curate, with a touch of sorrow in his words, "it is a heavy sin in you to speak so; there might be more charity on your tongue, even if your heart should grudge it; with such suspicions I have never served this cure."

Crispin felt he might have something answered this. "Would you have me learn to lie?"

"So I would not have you speak."

"Then you would that I lied the rather
to

to myself. No, father, the world may call this surface-loving that you so commend, and that it says it so believes in, charity. I would never hurt a hair of that man's head. So much may I hate; but for all that, and for a great deal more, I would not have her his. So much do I like to hate; if you ask me why and gave me hours to find a cause, perhaps I could not tell. If you ask me why the man who holds so many in a seeming spell keeps me away, I cannot tell. This great good man, who does his alms through a well salaried almoner, and his charities by some liberal commission, he does not need my words to mark his worth. Perhaps he is too good; but I do not think this Ruy Lyle would care to tell aloud his past on the highway."

"In that you have ill said, Crispin, and have liked to say it where you should have said nothing, you have said too much. It plagues me, Crispin, does the thought that this bitterness which grows so full may be your curse."

Crispin Ken had some reason to know
that

that his father would think him a very
long way cursed if he said more; so, whilst
he felt he could have answered a good
deal, he answered nothing; and the curate,
who perhaps saw what the concession
meant, bethought himself to ask whether
Crispin would go a little way to seek for
Jack.

"There are footsteps, father, coming
now;" and in another minute Jack's hand
was on the door.

"You are late, Jack," said the curate
with all the impatience of aggravated hunger
in his words, and who searched about to see
what Jack had brought. "What kept
you?"

"Mad Meg was out, and she is worth
the waiting for; for she is the one to get
the ticket. I watched for her a good time,
but she didn't come."

"Have you got nothing, then?" said
Crispin, who, for his father, almost seemed
to fear the answer.

"Haven't I? Is it for a fool that you
take me?" said Jack, beginning to un-
burden

burden himself, and casting off a good
deal of the little that was on him ; " but
they didn't like the coat so much, and had
a deal to say about the cloth."

" It is their business," said the curate ;
" they must live."

Reuben Ken did not like this thing to
be said against his cloth over a pawn ticket ;
and it quite seemed by what he said, and
from how he said it, that he had learned in
no long while a little of Crispin's want of
charity.

" They said, too, they didn't know you
were quite so hard up ; but though it
wasn't worth three shillings they didn't
mind a crown. Meg couldn't have bet-
tered that," said Jack, triumphantly.

" They are dissenters," muttered the
curate, who felt that in saying this he had
spoken the only commentary the thing
would bear, " and they will keep my coat ,
to show in chapel. I have conceded everything to them to come to this."

But a man who is so very near to starve,
when food is like again to touch his lips,
thinks

thinks all the less of means; and as Jack produced four of the longest candles they had seen for weeks, and hinted that there was a sack of coals in the shed, and showed a pound and a half of beef cut from the rump, and some potatoes, the curate came to see his way to spend his Christmas eve.

Jack sat down, and shook off the mist which was almost rain.

He was a cripple of perhaps fifteen years; but as with so many of the halt there was about his face that chiseling which so often is the birthright of the deformed.

"You didn't meet Mona, Jack?" said the curate. "I would have her here amongst us now," and Crispin looked into his father's face, and his father looked in his.

"I shall preach to-morrow, Crispin, if I live," said Reuben Ken as he sat up, and saw the grilling meat, and felt the fire. "I pray God that this gift of strength may last me over Christmas day."

"You have got no coat, father, you forget," said Jack; "but what's that?—there it is again,—if ever I did hear anything, I heard

heard Mona cry," and whilst he spoke the cripple struggled to the door.

"A light! a light! Mona's down," said the boy, as he took his sister in his arms.

"What's this place — where am I?" she tried to say, as after a little while she opened her eyes and looked round her.

They had laid her on the bed, and she sat up, and would have spoken, but as she came to know the faces by her, the tears welled over, and she buried her head on Crispin's breast.

"Some one followed me from the bottom of the lane, against the Hall, and kept getting nearer and nearer,"—and there was more a good deal in these words than at first might seem.

No one to harm had ever followed on the steps of Mona Ken for eighteen years. The very stocks would have been revived by the one voice of St. Hilda's—not often so unanimous—in favour of any one who by night or day should have molested her, and Jack sprung up as quickly as the straightest when he heard the words.

"You

"You, Mona, you — who — where ?"—
and the cripple ceased his hug around his
sister's neck, and had seized his hat and
crossed the door, when a woman stood
before him.

"Step aside, mother," said the boy, " I
have got work for this stick between here
and the Hall which won't bear waiting."

"Then you may put it up, Jack," said
the woman ; " it's work that will keep ; for
I take it you mean a mischief to some one,
and it was I who a bit since followed
Mona."

"You, mother ?" said the girl.

"You, Meg ?" said the curate and his
sons.

"You took a great liberty, then," continued Reuben Ken, "and it will be as
well you don't repeat it."

"Old friends may take them," said the
woman ; "and mustn't I be rough, girl, to
hold my title to Mad Meg ? But sure it
isn't worth so many words ; this is just how
it came about. I wanted to get to the Hall
before Mona left, but I was far away too
                                    late,

late, so I took a short cut over the field to
the bottom of the lane, and when she
heard me coming through the hedge yon-
der, she was scared like, and set to run-
ning; but Meg wanted a word with you,
Mona, and must have it yet, for the matter of that."

"It's all right, father," said Jack, who
was quite the chiefest friend of Mad Meg,
"*she* meant no harm."

"No, it isn't," said the woman, "and I
don't care who hears me say it; and right
it won't be either if Mona's to go to the
Hall at the bidding of the like of Ruy
Lyle."

"Do you know of whom you speak?"
said the curate, who began to think of all
the honours, parliamentary and philan-
thropic, which his neighbour bore.

"I ought to," said the woman with a
smile and an air which had gained for her
her name.

"He is quite the first man in the
county," said the curate.

"He prays a deal aloud, and knows a
good

good few people, and is known of a good few, but I don't know so much about his being first."

"Why, woman, you are living by his generous hand."

"I live on his third day's leavings," said Meg. "It's no business of mine, now, what he is; perhaps it may be, perhaps not; but Mona, you may not marry Ruy Lyle; that's just all I've got to say."

"Mother, I don't know what you mean."

"Jack," said the curate, "you are too familiar with this woman. Her madness grows too much. I cannot," continued the curate, addressing Meg, "hear you speak so of our common friend."

But Meg went on the rather, for she had come to speak, and would stay till she had out all her say.

"And so you are to go up to the Hall to-morrow?" said Meg, searching Mona's eyes; "and is it a dinner that John Wycherley will get there, too?"

"And do you forbid it?" said the curate, who

who but very little liked the woman's coming.

"Had I reckoned that my coming," said Mad Meg, "would have made you bitter, yet I should have come; and isn't it the time to speak before John Wycherley is put aside? Mona has given her love to him, and that welcome to the Hall just means —'cast Wycherley away!'"

"Woman, can't you see your words may wound?"

"I mean they should if there is a cause Girl, girl, you know how Mad Meg loves you!"

"It ill beseems you then to show it so," said the curate.

"The world is most civil when it lies," said Meg. "I did not ask for thanks when I should say that Ruy Lyle loves Mona."

"He has not sought her," said the curate, who meant by this that perhaps he would not mind it if his neighbour had.

"*That* man need not speak to ask for what he wants," said Meg; and in those words

words each one there saw the image of the owner of the Hall.

"Times must have altered," said the curate, "and altered for the worse, when the maid should ask the man."

As he spoke Mad Meg had reached the door, and lifting up her hand as she turned to go, she said to Mona, "Girl—girl, you may not marry Ruy Lyle!"

"Stay, stay," said the curate, "this is Christmas eve," and each one helped to ask Mad Meg to stay, for each one had a liking for that strange mad woman; but when Jack went out to seek her she was gone; and all seemed to think they heard those words borne up again beneath that advent sky,—"you may not marry Ruy Lyle!"

CHAP.

CHAP. II.

*How the Perpetual Curate of St. Hilda's
kept Christmas Day.*

IT was not in any way that the
perpetual curate of St. Hilda's
" cut his coat other than quite
according to his cloth," but that
the perpetual curacy did not make provision
for its perpetual curate wearing any coat
at all.

Reuben Ken had, under no very genial
circumstances, been parted from his coat
for the very inconsiderable consideration of
" a crown," when things had gone so hard
with him ; but if he was to preach to his
people on Christmas day, it was a settled

persuasion on his mind that it would beseem
his office best, to wear a coat.

" I shall preach to-day," said the curate—
who had not slept away his purpose, if he
could get anything to cover him—when
they met the next morning over such a
meal as was left from the last night's
supper.

" You had better not," said Crispin ; " it
is about the least wise thing that you can
do ;" and they all added something that
they hoped might so affect the curate's
purpose.

" It is not wise, I know that; but
something seems to tell me—something,"
said the curate, earnestly, " which I can
hardly disregard,—that I may not speak to
them again on any Christmas day."

" Father, you don't eat," said the cripple, sidling up with his own meat to tempt
his father.

Reuben laid his wasting hand upon the
cripple's head, and bade the boy take heart.

" I can't eat my own coat," said the
curate, smiling ; " it doesn't eat with a
relish,

relish, Jack. I wonder if he'd let me have it back to-day without the money?"

"I take it he would not," said Crispin; "he is too excellent a man of business. I think he would a great deal rather keep his pledge; though it well might be that a preaching pawnbroker may hope to be saved by his faith, he doesn't mean to trust the church."

"I hope he won't be leaving my coat about the shop," said the curate, apprehensively; "there would be no end to what might come of it. Don't you think he would let me have it for a couple of hours? Is he still so hard a man?"

The curate had eaten his own coat, and wanted yet again to eat it.

"I know he was glad enough to get it," said Crispin, "and I think he will be glad enough to keep it."

"He said a great many sermons might be preached about it," answered Jack, "and he thought he might say something that would tell."

"Did he, though?" moaned the curate,

who

who saw the peril. " I shouldn't wonder if he preached about it to-day. Wouldn't any one else have lent the money, Jack ?"

" The coat has got to be known, father ; you see it isn't as fresh as it was ; but *he* didn't mind giving a fancy price because he wanted it. He had a deal to talk about ; and wondered if the apostles were any better off than Curates."

" He attacks my authority through my coat," groaned Mr. Ken ; " and what did you say, Jack ? I hope you rebuked his irreverence ; he always had a hasty tongue."

" I asked him," answered Jack, smiling, " whether the extortioners in all ages were any worse off than the pawnbrokers in this."

" And what did he say to that, Jack ?" laughed the curate.

" He took it very gravely, and said that depended a good deal on whether competition was brisk for the pledges at the periodical sales. I asked him whether it wouldn't do if I brought him the coat to-morrow ; but he said he wasn't going to be

a different kind of man on Christmas day.
He had heard preachers of his own way of
thinking say, that if an angel was to come
down from heaven and want wrapping up,
that they shouldn't get anything warm
about them till they came down with the
money; that there was so much charity
nowadays, people couldn't be too cautious.
It was all very well for the shepherds to
leave their sheep and take to a star; if
people left their cattle about now they
were put in the pound, and quite right too.
He liked faith as well as any man, but it
wasn't trade to do without security. If
you will go to church, father, I think I can
manage to get you there."

"I am likely enough to get a chill, but
I shall go, God willing," said the curate.
"Perhaps that dissenter, to whom I taught
forbearance, thinks he can keep me away,
and that he will get my people to his
chapel because he has got my coat: but
perhaps I am hard upon the man."

The morning was wearing on, and there
was yet not a little to do. Jack had been

some

some time gone out, as it transpired later, to seek the friendly services of Mad Meg; and just after ten a servant from the Hall, a good deal decorated, came with a letter and a hamper, which he had, seemingly, not brought along to their delivery without a series of protests.

"I am to wait for an answer, please Miss," said the menial, as Mona opened the door.

"Sit you down," said the curate, and the man looked about as though it could never be that he was to be seated in the midst of a family, and wondered what sort of people they could be who invited him to sit amongst them.

The hamper quite betrayed the season : there was a sirloin, and a turkey-cock, and a ham, and a letter from the Hall. Mr. Lyle presented his compliments to the Rev. Reuben Ken, and hoped it would be agreeable for all at the curacy to give him the pleasure of their company at dinner, at six o'clock, that Christmas day. The sirloin, and the turkey-cock, and the ham Mr.

Mr. Lyle quite thought he might send to a perpetual curate with three children, and sixty pounds a year, without any more particular introduction.

"Mr. Lyle is very kind," said Crispin—who had some time seen what the hamper meant—addressing the servant; "and you will give him our compliments, but——"

"I think I should write a note," said Mona, blushing beyond what a note of thanks seemed to call for or explain.

"Do Mona, do," said the curate, who would have been more years in taking the measure of a neighbour than Crispin would have been minutes, "and tell Mr. Lyle, with my hearty thanks for his consideration, that it will give your brother and yourself much pleasure to dine at the Hall to-day. I have almost a mind to go myself."

"Father," said Crispin, who was not unaccustomed to see the curate carried away by a very little, "I do not think this wise, and neither is it just to Wycherley."

"What's that you are saying about me?" said John Wycherley, who was seemingly

not

not anticipating any very great injustice, getting to a chair by Mona's side; "but it's well that there's such cheer, for I mean to stay and dine."

John Wycherley's face fell a good deal when he heard from Mona's lips how matters stood; "but I shall not go now, John," said she, and the perpetual curate of St. Hilda's the less was comforted, as Crispin Ken thought, with too little caution.

"I would rather that you did, Mona," said her father, "we must not affront so good a friend."

"Never mind me, Mona," said Wycherley, who was struggling against showing how much he minded it; "I will dine with Jack and your father. Mr. Ken is right."

"That's just like you, John," said Crispin. "You wouldn't think it was right if you knew all; there, you are saying one thing because you want to think it is for the best, and can't believe it, whilst you are meaning another; you may mean to stay and dine, but you don't mean to stay and like it."

"I go to please my father," said Mona

to

to the curate of St. Hilda's the less, and
would a great deal rather dine with you,
John,"—and Wycherley's face grew bright
as he saw the smile on Mona's face; and
when Jack returned he found all well
pleased with the prospects of the day, all,
perhaps it should be said, but Crispin, in
whom had some time grown that very little
tolerated habit of saying what he thought.

"It's all right," said Jack, "Mad Meg's
done it;" and so it seemed, for drawn up
at the door was an old wheel-chair, in
which, tradition had it, that a former pro-
prietor of the Hall had died with some
suddenness one forenoon about a quarter
of a century before, and Jack, after leading
anticipation to a fitting pitch, produced
from it a brown coat, which, he said, the
pawnbroker let Meg have for half a crown.

The perpetual curate of St. Hilda's the
great looked aghast, as well he might,
when his youngest son held up that coat.
There was no better known coat in the
county. It had been advertised on the
backs of a succession of schismatics; it had

belonged

belonged to a non-conforming divine, a
sectarian leader, who liked as little as might
be the sect to which the pawnbroker belonged; so when that leader got into a strait,
and when the coat came to be pawned, the
pawnbroker felt there could be no room
more for his revenge.

"He thought it might fit you, father,"
said Jack, "but he says you must be quiet
in it."

"Does he think I should knock about
in it as he would?" groaned Reuben Ken.

It only wanted ten minutes to church
time; but no sensitive churchman could
have suffered so much to be put upon him,
in the putting on of such a coat without
resisting.

As the minutes moved on there was
nothing at all for him to do but hang it
about him. So the curate with a groan
suffered himself to be bound up in the cast-
off coat of schism.

"I don't think it's aired," said the curate,
who shuddered when he thought of what
his outward seeming was,—and the trials of
the

the Rev. Reuben Ken in no way abated, but they rather grew, as each new matter for his discomforting arose, and there seemed no chance of their avoidance. To get by the beadle,—to keep out the clerk,—but circumstances favoured the perpetual curate, and no man questioned him about his coat.

It had somehow so got about that Reuben Ken would preach, that the little church was full.

The perpetual curate of St. Hilda's the great, in the three-and-twenty years that he had been there, had drawn many to him who at one time had not been very strongly moved to be drawn to any preacher, and perhaps the distribution of what he had to say over no more than twenty minutes, had something very materially to do with the hesitating allegiance of all sorts towards him. Of late such curates as could be found had come there to take such liberties, as curates often will, and very many had been the experiments hazarded by all sorts and conditions of preachers.

Now, Reuben Ken, on whose want of

firmness,

firmness, and on whose want of method
the dissenters had builded much of their
success, hazarded nothing on this wise at
all.   He said " some people had more to
drink, and more to eat, and more to wear,
and more to make them glad than others
at those Christmas times; but," he said,
" those who had most now would not for
ever and for ever have everything in a great
way just as they had it then."   Reuben
Ken said this thing in a hard voice, for he
saw the pawnbroker, who he felt had come
to see him in that coat.   But all he said
till he stopped, though well to write upon
most hearts, would not read so well upon
this page.   He very simply told them what
the season meant.   It was not a popular
discourse at all.   He told them of all that
they might enjoy and yet live, and of all
they might indulge in and yet die.   He
said " that he had not escaped that year,
but that God had taken him out of the
shadows, and as they saw had made him
glad that Christmas.   He did not feel that
he should preach to them again.   They
                                        could

could see,' he said, "how hard it was for
him to fetch his breath, but it would be
harder to fetch soon. He had preached
to them there on one-and-twenty Christmas days. He was going to ask them to
take away with them such things as he
should have strength to say to them on the
morning of the last. He would thank
God, and they would thank God with him,
for what Christendom celebrated on that
day ; and they should none of them think
that they were a whit the less likely or less
favoured than their neighbours, whose coats
might have about them more of the fashion
of the season, and on whose plates might
be more of the season's gifts,"—and so he
urged them, "Let your living and your
lives connect you with a Christmas beyond
change."

There was nothing very new in this :
there was nothing new at all. It has been
said before from many of such places, and
on many of such days. With an easier air
it will be said again. But those who heard
those words spoken in that church took
them

them to their homes amongst the hills. The pawnbroker even, who had come to see how the curate acted in the coat, took a bit; and they had the meaning and the seeming of what would be last words; and whether that kindly hollow voice should speak again, there was a lingering, loving sound that would speak when it was still.

What little, Reuben Ken had said, he had fought against the want of breath to say; and now he leaned over the pulpit side and gasped a little, and it was seen that he was taking his last leave.

"I should tell you a lie, in this place, if I said that when I go from here I would the rather die; but I shall die soon. I want to meet you, every one, by and by up there; I want you to meet me there. Ask Him to give me, to give you, when it shall be His will, an undivided Christmas tide in heaven."

There was quite as great a gathering, — after the people had eaten their " last supper," with their pastor,—in the vestry as its resources well could hold.

Even

Even a sick man, on a Christmas day,
must smile and look pleasant over his share
of what, as the phrase has it, are the
" compliments of the season."

Now these compliments of the season,
in the most solid and the least transparent
circles, very often convey, in a measure,
more than they mean. But divers of these
neat-nothings were laid out on the perpetual curate, till that good and reverend
man thought he should have audience of
these talking folks for ever; he fancied
what was wished so well to him was real,
and perhaps it was, leastway, as much as
may be.

There was Mr. Lyle, and a little way
behind him, struggling to be seen, was
Miss Strake — Miss Aurelia Strake — the
maiden aunt of Mr. Lyle; and hitched up
in a corner, away by himself, was the
pawnbroker who preached.

Reuben Ken did not at all know what
this should mean, and thought the very
season might have softened down that man.

There was hardly ever any presence that
                                        could

could rival that of Ruy Lyle.   You could
never forget his eye; but you could
never exactly remember to have seen it
look you in the face.   It drew you near
but yet against your will.   When it had
been yours to feel what was the searching
fascination of his look, of his voice, of
his smile, somehow you would not reckon
the time tedious till you felt it again.
You would wonder why he could keep
his way and never seem to feel that anything went hard.   He was very pale, and
yet it did not seem he wanted colour;
he went softly, and yet it did not seem he
wanted strength; you would have given
a great deal to have asked him to look you
in the face, and yet, perhaps, you rather
grasped at his reserve.   He was not passion-
less, and yet you never saw him set aside
that smile.   Nothing seemed too much
for him to have with equanimity; nothing
seemed too much for him to go without
with equal equanimity.   That silvered hair,
silvered on no more than forty years, and
that silver beard, and that oval face were
not

not the hair, or the beard, or the face
of a man who had just come to his prime.
You may have seen some such a face
accredited, in a missal, to an elderly saint,
or figured out on a cartoon. You would
never have felt more at ease in your life
than at his table, whilst you would never
remember to have felt more powerless to
take his depth.

Ruy Lyle was member for the county
on " Liberal " principles ; and no man
could leave him " across country ;" if he
was not always at the front, it was felt
that even he might well be tired of always
excelling. No one who ever witnessed
what was not a lie, could say that his alms
were not a younger son's inheritance ; there
had been a great many theological parties
started in that cure, but Ruy Lyle became
at once a centre ; it was felt that only
what he liked could live. No one ever
realised that high churchmanship was con-
demned, because he made low churchmanship possible alone. Ruy Lyle had
come there and had settled down a mystery ;
and

and if you had been minded to taste and
to explain him, you would have felt what
others felt, and passed the riddle on.

Mr. Lyle that Christmas morning
took the curate's hand, as Reuben Ken,
surprised with such congratulations, had
hurried off his coat, and Mr. Lyle said,
" my dear Mr. Ken, to hear you preach
was such an unexpected pleasure—we shall
see you at dinner by and by—and you,
Mr. Wycherley—no ceremony ; we shall
be quite alone."

The only one Mr. Lyle could be said
to have asked with his eyes—but no one
could avouch they saw them raised—was
Mona. His eyes did not meet her's, but
she felt that he had asked her only.

" Crispin and Mona will realise your
hospitality, my good friend," said Reuben
Ken ; " but Jack and Mr. Wycherley will
stay and keep me company."

Mr. Lyle bowed, so that it was hard to
say—hard as it always was—whether he
was well pleased or whether he took the
refusal roughly. No one could account
for

for what he meant or said, though some told how that he had sharp pains near his heart, and so was strange.

Miss Strake, who looked crisper than the weather by more than a degree, repeated, as though extemporaneously, what it was fitting and regular for a gentlewoman managing a large establishment to repeat on Christmas day ; and she said, "she hoped Mr. Ken would have a merry Christmas, and many of them."

Now, Miss Aurelia Strake, when she so spoke that pleasant thing, had quite the means of knowing that Mr. Ken had one lung and no coat.

"My dear lady, I shall hope it may be a merry one," said the curate, as well as the one lung would let him, " for I have some time felt that it would be my last."

"That it certainly will," said the maiden aunt, ominously — with that sort of overdone pantomime which should have passed for a reproof, and holding up, what some consumptive man with expectations some five-and-twenty years before had called her little

little hand,—" and that you will bring
upon yourself, Mr. Ken, if you stand in
the cold without your coat."

" My dear lady, your interest is very
grateful, you are very kind, but——"

" Oh! do let me assist you, Mr. Ken.
I can't let you do it,—it will make you
cough; after your sad illness, Mr. Ken,
your people will not let you risk your pre-
cious life. We young folks can do anything; you should never be without your
coat this weather."

Miss Strake, this may be the proper
place to say, had heard of the coat's
vicissitudes and change of pla.e and circumstances, and thought this little em-
barrassment would not clash very materially
with the compliments of the season.

" My dear lady, indeed I cannot let you
wait any longer. There has been a little
mistake. I seem to—have come—to—to
—church in—in a coat that was strange
to me. I—I——"

" Your coat is come, sir," said the pawnbroker, reappearing at a crisis not to the
liking

liking of Miss Strake, and as he left the coat upon the curate's arm, Reuben seemed to feel the pressure of that erratic tradesman's hands.

"It's all right," said the pawnbroker, leading Mr. Ken aside, "there's nothing to pay; but I couldn't bear to hear you talk like that of dying, and think you hadn't got a coat; I havn't done you any good I know for two-and-twenty years; but there's an end of that now, Mr. Ken. It isn't too late for me to say it, is it? You ain't going to die; if you'd been a bit more firm that Sunday about the singing and the surplice, I shouldn't have been the 'light' I've been at Meeting,—but don't you talk of dying now."

The curate who in those minutes lived those two-and-twenty years again, tried very hard indeed to stop him; but the pawnbroker had more in his heart than he could stifle, and the glad curate brushed away the dew of joy.

Reuben Ken pressed Mr. Lyle as much as it was well to press such a neighbour to

stay

stay and have some lunch; but Mr. Lyle
had all the tact to stay away, and at six
o'clock Crispin and his sister sat down to
dinner at the Hall.

There was no one asked to meet them.
Miss Strake, who was dressed like a young
girl, presided, and looked quite her best—
and Miss Strake did not throw away her
best on all.   The dinner was served on
silver gilt, and there were two servants in
livery about the table, and one who was
not seen, outside the door.   This was perhaps more than enough, but of what was
set before them there was more than enough
too.   The best that Ruy Lyle could offer
was quite the best the county could provide,
with London to complete the competition.

Mona, who had never dined at the Hall
before in Mr. Lyle's time, thought that of
the courses there would never be an end;
and the splendour of the room, and the
presence of her host, seemed like a spell, as
very well it might, about her.   He poured
out all the power of his conversation, and
Mona felt, as she sat there with that magnificence

nificence about her in a stuff gown, rather
" skimpy," that it was like nothing she had
ever heard or seen before—it perhaps rather
awed her—it held her in a chain of wonder;
and yet when afterwards his words rose up
again she could not think of anything that
did not please her. He asked her to take
wine with him, but he did not raise his
eyes; and Miss Strake, who had been at
intervals drawing Crispin out, and had
talked of " Mamma," and had told him that
it would be so nice if she could only walk
about and see the country, but that
"Mamma" did not think well of young
people walking about alone, said, " by the
by, do you know I was afraid Mr. Ken
might have lost a coat; for I had heard
that one of his had been seen at the pawnbroker's; of course the rumour never went
beyond me ? "

Mr. Lyle saw that this gave pain, and
changed the subject, without any one seeing
how it had been changed; and some time
after tea, as Mona had said how much she
should like to see every thing that Mr.
Lyle

Lyle had introduced into the Hall, the host ordered up a hand lamp, and offered to show her through the palace he had reared.

Mona had read about fairyland, and the regular allowance of enchanted castles, but in this fashion she had never read that things so beautiful could be.

She seemed to walk, as they passed from chamber to chamber, on acres of velvet pile; and Mona marvelled, as much as might be, where this magnificence would end.

Ruy Lyle, too, in such a scene seemed well to form a part of it. He looked like one of the pictures Mona remembered to have copied once out of the "Acts of the Apostles."

"You are tired, Miss Ken, and you have as much more to see."

They were alone; Miss Strake was in the long drawing-room talking about her schoolfellows, and other young subjects.

Mona sat down, and as she drank in all she saw she would have liked to have enjoyed it her own way. Her stuff dress she fancied grated on the damask silk.

"Do

"Do you approve the alterations, Miss Ken?" asked Ruy Lyle, in a tone which seemed to say, if you don't they only remain until something more successful to succeed them can be organised.

Mona did not see that the enchanter himself had sat down on the amber silk beside her.

"It is a palace for a king," she said, musing in her innocence, and looking up and down the sumptuous vista.

"And of which could you be queen?" asked Ruy Lyle, on his knees, at her feet.

"If you please, Miss Mona, Mr. Ken isn't so well; taken a chill he thinks this morning; and I thought it likely you might wish to know," and none other than Mad Meg stood before them.

Mona started, not more perhaps at the woman's sudden coming than at what Ruy Lyle had asked her. What did that question mean? But Mad Meg was at some pains that there should be, at least that night, no explanation.

Mona Ken no longer remembered what

Ruy Lyle had asked her when she reached her home that night. She could face John Wycherley with as little guile, as she so guileless, ever had. Her smile was the same —as bright, as soft. Her father searched her eyes, but saw no change. What she felt for Lyle, and whatever she might come to feel, had nothing in it of the love she felt for Wycherley.

And did it last? Might he who had not always that which he could wear, be set in the balance with the owner of those velvet acres? Might he who could only say, " be my wife, be one with nothing," ask, and before him have, who could say " be my queen?" Did the leaven of that invitation work, which said so softly, " reign with me?"

Where the charitable have swollen into the biggest crowds, there shall she be adjudged false before they turn this page.

CHAP.

CHAP. III.

Reuben Ken—A Catastrophe " on 'Change."

BLOOD is as material to begin a chapter as to found a race. There is, and always has been, quite as little liking as may be, to the creation of fiction of doubtful blood. The long pedigree goes a great way to get rid of the prejudices against a short purse. It were better that the parvenu never came to the birth, than that by accident he should at some time bleed. The curse in his veins should course unseen. It is not well to think too little of this blood just now. A good deal of it abroad is no more royal than is any of the ornamental water in the parks, and about as little clean. A great yield of corruption taints them both.

D 2

This

This blood, it cannot be confounded when you get it clean; but something else than pedigrees are wanted in an age of penny fares. Blood serves England still; the substitute more likely serves itself. All blood has not its heroes, nor have all heroes blood. When the pride of blood first mounted to a price, it something did beseem the bloodless, to hang about his skin what men of blood should wear. What specialities remain for blood, when nearly all the world has found equality in sixteen-shilling trousers?

Reuben Ken, so far as blood was his, was not ill-found. His mother, who had been an heiress, and bargained away—, sickening of the bargain—had died young, seeming not to care at all to live.

Richard Ken, for whom she had been set aside over a stoup of wine by her father, before she was well weaned, objected nothing. It was likely, then, that she was set on making up her mind to want to die. There is something very common in those things. A man who had lived away his liver,

liver, and discounted the power of his
prime, had married her, because everything had been arranged that they should
be married decently, so that blood and
money might be got together—the blood
it certainly seemed meeting the settle-
ments quite half-way; and out of this
arrangement they were got to the altar on
a certain day, " before God," as the divine.
who was in the secret of the sale, would
have it.

But no one of those, who were gathered
there about them, thought that that was
such a lie; it did not look the thing it
was. It is often done, and no one ever
seems to wonder; but everybody hoped,
and put up the sound aloud, " they would
be happy," which to many had much of
the exceeding freshness of an afterthought.
And when blood and money had been decently seen into a chariot, with a heavy
weight on the near-side grey horse, with a
new satin jacket—quite a suggestion it
should be said of blood, but as entirely a
provision of money—the two rather elderly

gentlemen

gentlemen who had managed it all up to
that point, without, they thought, being
suspected to have done a very little business, came back and exchanged many civil
salutations, and took wine one with the
other, and blood had quite the worst of it.
But the papers—some of the gentlemen
from which received considerable attention—spoke of it in their next issue in a
sort of serious way that was the most
proper and reverential; and the whole
thing as it was seen looked really very well.

Richard Ken, as years went on, came to
have three children ; but two—he thought
by some special mercy, as he looked upon
them in their little coffins—were carried
away young.

Reuben Ken was the heir, and how he
came to be so called Reuben was something
on this wise.

Richard Ken saw life, and saw his friends
with the money he had married.

Richard Ken had shown, as early as
might be, that his highest instincts would
lie in the direction of speculative accumu-
lation.

lation. As a little lad he would race his own tabby against the neighbour's big black cat, and get the odds on the issue in four-penny pieces. Such a soul—and courtesy has declared for the presence of a soul—to do itself the merest justice, if he was spared to be a grown up gambler, could only lead one way; and it was decided to devote such unmistakable promise to the Stock Exchange.

Richard Ken, basing his operations on the models about him, had always thought a good deal of making money, and, perhaps less in proportion than he might have, how he made it. But he was going in for a great game; and the great game is to be builded up, as near as decency permits, to where some other speculator has been spilled.

Before he was thirty he cared for nothing that was in all the world, and that was beyond the world—and he expected to find specie in another place—but money.

He only knew men, and was only seen about with men, who had money, or who

were

were coming into money ; none that had had money, and had lost that money. And amongst those whom he had been a great while trying to know, and at last had got to know, was one Reuben Israel ; and what he felt was ever so much better, Reuben Israel did not deny that he knew him.

Reuben Israel was the greatest judge of " paper" in the world. He had done something to keep every power in Europe in credit ; and sometime or another had stood between them and bankruptcy.

He only took up the biggest loans ; such loans as everybody else together that the Bank parlour could hold, found it hard to take up.

What he was worth, at his best, no one ever knew. He did not know himself. He had once kept ten clerks to ascertain it ; but such a calculation did not come within the grasp of finite means. One after the other the ten clerks died away, and those that were last were many millions off from the end.

Next to making money, it was the business

business of the natural life of Richard Ken
to get to know this Reuben Israel.

One day Reuben Israel met Richard
Ken, and the man of loans was seen by
many credible witnesses—just under where
some satirist has declared over the heads
of the gentlemen of the Stock Exhange,
"That the earth is the Lord's, and the
fulness thereof"—for some forty and five
minutes to talk to Richard Ken.

From that day till he died, Richard Ken
talked in no wise for forty and five minutes
together to any one other than to the man
of loans. Every one thought there was
something in it, but no one quite knew
what it all should mean. If Richard Ken
did "operate" for less than his half-crown
a hundred, others "on 'change" might be
persuaded to do like him. Some one said
that Reuben Israel did his best things on
Sunday, and that Richard Ken did not
much care to go to church. But all
gentlemen of the Stock Exchange are not
always to be found in their pews on the first
day of the week, between eleven and one

o'clock ;

o'clock; and others said that Richard Ken
knew of something that Reuben Israel did
not care should see the light. But it was
not held to be at all likely that a man, who
did not know what he was worth, would
let anything see the light that he did not
choose should see it. He would not feel
the need of buying up a broker.

No one ever did know; and at last
" What is Richard Ken to Reuben Israel "
was asked as hopelessly as who wrote
Junius's Letters. It always ended in the
one distress, and in the one belief, that
" the devil only knows."

It is not unlikely that he did. All that
the world knew in general was that they
did everything together; and all that it
ever knew in particular was, that Reuben
Israel, who had been taken in the right
humour, was to be godfather to the heir of
Richard Ken.

Reuben Israel, who was now Sir Reuben,
as he well might be, had never been known,
under any pressure, to stand for any Christian infant before. No few of these Christian
infants

infants had been brought up to tempt him ;
but the heir of Richard Ken was somehow
quite the first to get him.

Sir Reuben Israel did something more
than take upon himself just the necessary
compliment of the Christian profession. In
consideration of the infant taking his
name, Sir Reuben Israel indicated his inten-
tion of seeing him sometimes through the
world ; and there was every necessary indication of what this should mean. Reuben
Ken would get his "paper" "done" easily,
no matter how the market ruled ; and
there would be ever so much more in this
than in being asked whether he were " N
or M."

Other than this, the coming of Reuben
Ken to the font was much the sort of decent
desecration that such comings often are.
A good deal of christianity, that it would
not be held charitable to impugn, is got
together after such a fashion.

Reuben Israel said all the responses with
affecting earnestness ; but perhaps just a
little as if he were feeling his way into

some

some unexplored novelty. It might have been set down, by people who are critical, as a formal insult to his God; but then what a city connection it cemented! and then everything was done so very decently.

Ever since the day that Reuben Israel and Richard Ken had had that forty-five minutes' understanding Mr. Richard Ken had been a rising man. He left St. John's Wood at a sacrifice of a quarter's rent. He tried Tyburnia, and sent his footman one Wednesday morning to treat for a front pew. It was quite Mr. Richard Ken's experience that going to church, as he went, looked " rather well." Perhaps the service did begin a little early, but there was no better place, he found, for family men to draw him out on safe investments, than outside the church door.

After awhile Mr. Richard Ken bought himself an estate in Cumberland, and once Sir Reuben Israel was got there to stay out a week.

Richard Ken had sometime buried his wife,

wife, with every sumptuous form of sepulture. His allegiance to her memory was not by any means equivocal. He refrained himself from "'Change" for several days during a monetary crisis, whilst the body was about; but during the intervals of his getting above his sorrow, when he could be so approached, his clerk came to take his instructions, and nothing much was lost. So that fifteen years' mistake was buried in three coffins out of sight.

Reuben Ken was just as little like his father as might be; and their sympathies were on no better terms. Reuben had seen, when he was brought down in velvet after dinner, ever so much too much of his father's city friends to care at all to live as they lived; but when he put that velvet by, and could take the measure of those friends, he very much cared to live as they did not.

Sunday night was the great night at Mr. Richard Ken's. One or more reputable brokers always passed it with him; and some of the best things that were current
" upon

"upon change" came of these Sunday orgies.

If Mr. Richard Ken was never very faithful to his wife, it was but little likely he would be to her memory; and he was not faithful even before his only son.

Richard Ken never drank; no one ever saw him over-set with wine. He could not calculate in wine. He calculated it was so much income to him what he got out of those who did drink; so with Richard Ken, Sunday never ran to waste. He thought it better to be dry, and there was no saying, so he said, "what might then be got beyond the ruling prices." Could he have got this the easier for drinking, Richard Ken would have drunk; but he plied those who came to him as friends, and filled his pocket by their shame.

Reuben's education had not taught him to think highly of his father. Mr. Richard Ken thought indifferently well of public schools. So far as he understood them he believed they might do well enough for bishops' sons. Thank God his was not a
bishop's

bishop's son. Mr. Richard Ken desired
that Reuben should be kept away from such
contamination. He had a great many of
the regular prospectuses ; but one gentleman, whose terms were represented as
merely nominal, and who did everything
for a very little, was the one selected, from
considerations other than those which were
wholly educational.

After he had sought out, with a sort of
affectionate interest—which, if sufficiently
common, is not commonly reproved—Reuben's age, and had got to learn what his
pupil took to and refrained himself from,
he asked Mr. Ken whether he thought
the money market just then very healthy.

Mr. Richard Ken always asked this of
himself every morning fasting, before he
even said his prayers ; and his prayers came
to be long, or short, or nothing, as circumstances answered it. Beyond this the cheap
educationist, who knew the city man's weak
point, said, "That he had committed all
that he had," which might not have meant
much, to some popular debenture stock.

Mr.

Mr. Richard Ken rather believed in debenture stock; he believed in it as much as a man who suspects everything can believe in anything; and so the education of Reuben Ken was on this foundation.

When he was fifteen his father showed him at dinner every Sunday to his Sunday friends; and his father thought the time had about come when his heir should be started to make money in the world.

Indeed, it had long been clear to Mr. Ken that his son could only be one thing, unless he were a fool; but it eventuated to the father's thinking that Reuben Ken was a very fool, on a sort beyond all fools known.

The thing began with an affectionate interview, and ended with a commercial imprecation.

" Reuben, I shall be glad to have a word with you; those ' Turks,' which have been up and down all the morning, are not very firm, to be sure, and I should like to watch them, but you are getting old enough to help me; " and so Richard Ken, with his

Turks

Turks out of sorts, put aside the first five minutes out of fifty years to advise his son.

"You are quick at figures I hear; you wouldn't be any use here if you were not; but you don't want to go back to school."

There was hypocrisy in this opening, for Richard Ken had never heard of any boy who did.

"Not to that school if you don't like it; it is well enough, but I am too young for college yet."

"Too young for what? I didn't catch the word."

"I said I thought I might be over young for college."

"Reuben, you're a fool. I see it all; I have begotten a fool! College! College, boy! you don't get into working order for ''Change' there, I take it; college! if you mean anything, you mean the workhouse. Why Sir Reuben Israel never went to college, and he could buy up the Universities, only he knows better than to touch such drugs; you'll learn more here in a week than at college in a life; why, I could teach

what

what you call college a good deal. Just
look at this; I was offered twenty thousand
to give that fellow Dross's son a share, a
fourth, a fifth, anything I might like; but I
wasn't such a fool as to like anything. I
wasn't going to let him into a corner of
this concern, eh ! Do you take ? "

" I hope you did not keep it for me. I
do not think that I should like it."

" I don't suppose you would; like isn't
the word. Why, boy, I paid that fellow the
little he was worth, and so much extra, to
teach you the value of money. I shall not
hear you; you don't know what you're saying; you will be sorry for this when you're
cool. I don't ask you what you fancy;
when you're as old as I am you will fancy
nothing else."

Reuben Ken was not the boy to show
that he thought ill of such a father; perhaps he was tried a little over much, but
he only said, " I think I have made up my
mind to go to college."

Mr. Richard Ken never exhibited all his
resources at once. He always had something

thing in reserve; so he gathered himself up, as he knew the time was come when he should do it, looked round to see that nothing could come of the doors being ajar, and whispered, " Why, boy, do you know what I'm worth ? "

Reuben Ken, who had known his father more or less for nearly sixteen years, by certain tests that sons of city men should not hold up too severely, quite thought that he could tell; but Mr. Richard Ken left his son no time to think about it.

" Why, Reuben, I was worth two hundred thousand pounds when I realised upon the last account, and I'm not poorer now than I was then. I have only one son, and he may get to have all, but I can have no college : you must be a man of business."

" And if I say I would rather go to college."

" I shan't believe you, sir ; no one would say so—no one who was fit to be at large; no one would throw away two hundred thousand pounds."

" But I don't want the money."

" Yes,

"Yes, you do; yes, you do, every one wants money—not a little money—what's the use of a little money? It's very well for those parsons who talk against money. Why, I've heard them have the face to tell a church full of sound men, whose paper I know I'd discount, that a beast of a camel—a thing with a hump—could get through a needle's eye, more likely than that they would get to heaven. Why can't they talk what's written in the Bible instead of saying what they think. There is nothing about camels and needles in the Bible. God forbid that you should ever be a parson."

"I shall be that or nothing," answered Reuben.

"That's right enough," answered his father; "if you're a parson, boy, you will be nothing; it all comes of going to church. Don't talk in this way, or I'll tell you what it is, I shall give up my pew."

"And if I go to college, and if I do take orders?"

"Orders!

" Orders ! Take what, sir ?—you don't call doing business here taking orders, do you ? I'm no tradesman, sir. What do you mean ?"

Reuben could not help a smile as he explained what he had meant.

" You will not have the two hundred thousand pounds if you do, or any part of it."

" I do not ask it," answered Reuben, mildly. " I do not say I do not want it, or that I should well like to see it given to others, but I do say I would not have it, or a pound of it, on your terms."

" If you are serious," said Richard Ken, who had never in all his life heard any one talk so lightly of two hundred thousand pounds, " tell me as much as you like of this again to-morrow. I believe you are very mad ;" and at that time the next day Reuben Ken, in the little parlour over against Throgmorton Street, said it all again.

His father, when he could collect his senses and realise that he was so spoken

to

to by his own son, was moved to tell him he should have a thousand pounds when he should ask it ; and he had his attorney in that same afternoon, and made another will, and wiped clean out his own son's name.

Richard Ken was quite persuaded now, that his own son was very mad.

Reuben Ken for some three years returned to school, and then graduated in honours at Balliol College, Oxford. After that, for awhile he lived there as a tutor, and then married, as his father always said he would, the daughter of a farmer, a statesman on the Cumberland border.

Edith Dane came to him with nothing; and when Richard Ken heard it in his parlour one day when things were very flat, he wrote a letter to his son, and said that if he ever saw him again he should begin to think his own capacity for business was not what it used to be ; and when Reuben Ken wrote to his father the letter came back to him unopened.

The city man did what he said he would,
and

and Reuben Ken never saw his father in this world again.

It was a little later that Reuben Ken, who throughout, as he had never appealed against his father's curse, had never brought himself to say one word against his father, but was busied to soften down, what to himself seemed hard, was presented with the perpetual curacy of St. Hilda's the great, a preferment lying on the borders of Cumberland and Westmoreland, with eight hundred souls, and sixty pounds a year.

But they were beginning; and in looking forward were not much stricken by what they could look back on, and so they took it hopefully; Edith, the while, much comforting him that such a net incoming every year, would go some way : and with her loving thrift it did.

Mr. Richard Ken had now got to be so nearly the first man on 'Change that he had only to live, it was reckoned, about six months more to be so; but as some one preaching, on his sudden going, phrased it, " he fell asleep " the second best.

Mr.

Mr. Richard Ken, one morning in May, was " a bear ; " and public securities had taken such a turn as to leave him with no little apprehension as to the " account."

Things got worse, and so much worse, that the broker never went to bed at all. Thirty-six hours he knew would leave him where he was, or see out the end of his credit.   He did not care to face this last contingency ; but for the second best man it was really very near.

Richard Ken, after having passed an hour at noon, in the little room with Sir Reuben Israel, went out with a face that was long, — for all that he could do to make it hide his thoughts—" on 'Change," to think ; and he took counsel with him-self till it was nearly three, when some one saw him put his hand upon his side and fall.

A dozen hands were there to pick him up and set him on his legs, but he shook them off, and crawled under one of the seats and groaned.   It was a bad thing for the second best man to have come to.

" I

"I shall be better presently," he gasped; "I am well enough here."

What those curious ones around him thought was very different. It was ill for such a man to be gasping out the little life that was left, under a side seat upon 'Change.

"Send for a physician," said one, who had a reason for his humanity.

"I have sent for three," said a gentleman, who had three reasons for his, and who seemed perhaps a little over anxious to keep Mr. Richard Ken by any artificial means alive, and was unloosing the broker's cravat.

"Leave my throat alone," moaned Richard Ken, whose instinct, just then at fault, told him that they wanted his life; "and if you've been fools enough to send for any doctor, you may pay him, I shan't. It's a great liberty to take with the pockets of people of whom you know nothing. I'm only a little faint; but,"—continued Mr. Ken more blandly—"could any one just tell me what consols are at now?"

The friend who had sent for the three

physicians was a " bull." Indeed the group around the stricken, man were mostly " bulls."

" Do his friends know it, because they ought ? " said the doctor who had first arrived ; " he may live ten minutes. I can't give him more."

" So sudden !" said a clergyman who was passing by, and had taken the dying broker by the hand. " God grant that he may be prepared to go to his account ! "

" And what's that to you, whether I'm prepared for the account ;—who said I wasn't ;—whose taking away my credit in this place ? "

The three physicians had arrived ; they shook their three heads ; that was all they could do.

" Can he be made to live six-and-thirty hours ? " asked some one, more officious and feeling than the rest, and who thought he well might discount the " event ;" " and then be got to sign a check ? "

The three physicians thought it would be long over in as many minutes.

" I

" I say, don't let this get into the evening papers," groaned Richard Ken, now frothing at the mouth, " I shall only want time to save my credit,—only time,—time—" But Richard Ken was beyond all time then.

The fitting means of burying such a man, were to have pulled up a flag and put him under the Exchange ; but there was no precedent for this, and there was no power.

When it got to be known, that everything which Richard Ken possessed had been lost to Sir Reuben Israel, his memory was proportionately so much the less at a premium. " After hours " " it was operated in," at a discount.

The hardest quite believed, according as they had " been hit," that his soul would get it hot; but this comfort even was denied to those who would lay odds he had no soul at all.

CHAP.

CHAP. IV.

Edith of St. Mona.

MR. Richard Ken's memory, as quite beseemed such a reverential belonging in a " bear," was buried in chief in the money article. But Mr. Richard Ken, without much warning, and without telling those whom it most concerned, had gone away out of the world during a crisis, and had died worth nothing. There was not so much to be said for a man whose end had been on such a fashion, no matter what immunities city morals could plead. To take it at the best, it certainly was something to have died in a corner upon 'Change, — to have had three physicians with a different diagnosis, none of whom were ever paid, about him, — to have had the minutes — it was made a business — he

should

should live betted on and against; and where he should go to when he came to die, offered, with any number of takers.

Everybody had always struggled for some of his "paper." He was the only man in whose ear Sir Reuben Israel, when his confidence was at its most, ever whispered. That such an one should die just worth so many pennies in the pound, whose estate, at the fullest stretch, offered but a shabby yield of fourpenny-pieces!

It was very bad; and some pious people went so far as to get a moral out of it— rather against the city. But they found the city offered any number of just such morals; so they gave up the inquiry, in lack of strength to carry it on. How could a money article be pleasant, or anything but grievous, with the memory of such a "leading description" that had come to so much grief?

Mr. Richard Ken was buried in a shell, as near the top of the ground, as the rules of the ground would warrant. The undertaker had to do it for so much; and the

SO

so much happened to be but a ghostly little of the attenuated dividend. Mr. Richard Ken was shovelled away by contract into four feet four of a clay soil.

Sir Reuben Israel was very adequately represented by one of his coachmen, and by one of his carriages. There were no mutes; and no one there who represented his credit, to offer gratuities to the thirsty bearers of his body. Those gentlemen said it was about the very driest thing they ever did; and if the curses of the quick, in the employ of the funeral contractor, can touch the dead, the dust of Richard Ken did not rest well.

How he had stood, when he had fallen down upon that flag with his God, affected none; but how he had trifled with "the House" grew into quite a popular concern. So the burying of his body was of the fifth class; some five pounds fifteen in all— discount five per cent. for ready money. Bitterest satire was the ready coin.

Reuben Ken, in his little parish in the north, saw the summing up of his father's fame

fame in the money article, and was some
time full of hearty sorrow, that he who had
hated, and had never ceased to curse him,
had so died. For it is not well that this
sorrow should be taken away from the sons
of men, and the peril of a child's eternity
be left to rest too surely on those from
whose loins they spring ; or even city
circles may be got to learn in " after hours "
that, where their credit is quoted at a premium, more souls by it will be accredited
to hell, than by the other thousand means
which rule the market.

Society starts back with all its sickly affectation, and mouths of want of "charity,"
when it is told in words it does not like to
hear, of fathers " very generally respected "
lying on big beds, choking, as they roll from
side to side, with the half ripe curse that
would have asked damnation on a son,
because that son would follow something
nobler than his father loved.

It was so with the father of Reuben
Ken. The boy thought more highly of
Oxford than he did or could of Capel

Court :

Court; more of the cure of souls than
of consols; and he was cursed so long as
ever there was breath to curse him with.
But saved from the wreck of Paradise
is the love, with which the child would
seal a kiss upon the foul-mouthed lips that
fret to curse him.

From a very boy, Reuben Ken had never
been so much moved to take a part and
hold it. That he should have declared so
unhesitatingly for the Church, and summoned up his strength to stand by it, was,
perhaps, quite the first time he had kept
on his way, till he heard the words of his
own father cast him out of his inheritance,
because he had thought more of the cure
of souls than of price currents.

The estate of Richard Ken in Cumberland had stood near the acres of a yeoman,
one Caleb Dane; and perhaps the liking
of the two near neighbours for each other
was just about as little as might be.

When Richard Ken, by the countenance
of Sir Reuben Israel, had got to be well to
do, and Caleb Dane the rather less abounded

in

in his means, the time was critically judged
to have come when Mr. Richard Ken believed he might like to hate his neighbour
with no small advantage. The ill feeling
came of about a dozen roods or less of
freehold land, which were the property
of Caleb Dane, and which Richard Ken
a good deal wanted for his own. Caleb
Dane held it at first against all offers, because he rather liked the land, and for any
time after that, perhaps, because of human
nature, as he saw how much his neighbour
was angered by his purpose.

When Mr. Richard Ken was creeping
up, and had begun to get a name in city
circles that was considered practically to
mean a reputation, it was thought by that
gentleman that, under pressure, Caleb Dane
could be tempted to give up the land.

Mr. Richard Ken, after a little thinking,
put the matter in the sort of light he did
most things, when he was bargaining with
men of little substance—he always began
by being over civil.

" It's a niceish piece of land, Mr. Dane,

and

and a nice clean soil." Mr. Ken had been told by a seedsman in the city, who largely took him in, that he was a great judge of soils. " Come, now—anything in reason."

"I'm very sorry, Mr. Ken, but it doesn't seem to suit me to sell it."

And it no longer suited Mr. Ken to be civil.

" Oh, if it don't suit you, Mr. Dane, there's an end of it ; of course that's your affair ; you know best whether you most like the land or the money ; but I had heard," continued Richard Ken, in the tone he adopted in the city when he wanted something a point under the market price, " I *had* heard you wanted a little ready money ; but perhaps it's just as well; for some people do say it's poor stuff after all—poor stuff, Mr. Dane—a sort of spot likely enough for a manure heap ; but that would be a nuisance to me."

Mr. Dane said nothing, but it cost a good deal in his inner man to say nothing. He had never done a dirty thing in his life ; but with such words cast at him he felt

felt as a man would feel who had never
done a dirty thing ; and it was very little
he liked to be told that any one had heard
he wanted ready money. Perhaps he felt
his horny hand for a moment tighten on
his stick. But the city man was not worth
that.

Caleb Dane within him knew what he
should do.

The next morning when Mr. Richard
Ken cast his longing eyes upon the bit of
land, he saw a dung heap standing like a
cone upon the field. Mr. Richard Ken
could ill find cause to quarrel because of
his very own idea.

Ever after this, one of those who Richard
Ken gave up to his whole hate was Caleb
Dane.

It was some three years later that
Reuben Ken, who had been presented
with the perpetual curacy of St. Hilda's
the great, the parish in which the estates
of Richard Ken and Caleb Dane were
placed, came to live amongst the people
he had known as a boy. When it was

told,

told, as it soon was, how his father had cast him off, many were the right honest hearts much gladdened by his coming, and no one shook his hand more heartily than Caleb Dane.

The perpetual curacy of St. Hilda's the great, was no very considerable ecclesiastical preferment. It was not meant for any man to marry on. The church,—which, in the benevolence of those who built it, was only designed for the coming together of a very limited number of souls at separate seasons—is one of the oldest Norman relics left in England. The curacy offered just enough to make starvation a very reasonable and possible prospect. There were, it was reckoned, when population was at its best, about eight hundred souls within the cure. And never, perhaps, in so little space, had ever come together so many sorts of big men.

Sixty pounds is hardly over much to give eight hundred souls a decent sort of care. The district was peopled with miners; for the curacy of St. Hilda's the great

great offered to one of the largest lead
mines in Cumberland, the only church
within many miles. It is not at all hazarded here, in the interests of correct
chronicling, that at the very best and
soberest of times more than a spare fourth
of the eight hundred ever went to church.
But the attendance, it was pleaded, and
not it would seem without some cause,
was materially affected by its being bad
to sit two hundred. Neither men nor
women—except at fashionable chapels,
where there is a fashionable preacher, and
what is gone through is of the nature of
a performance—ever care to stand; and
this was just the difficulty of Reuben Ken,
as it had been of those who had gone
before him, but had cared a great deal less
about it.

"Why don't you come to church?"
was what he asked the great majority of
the astonished three fourths who stayed
away, before he had been among them a
week.

"If we was all to come, it would like
to

to be in one another's laps; it wouldn't be much of the sort of what you people call the house of God to see a lot of hundreds of the size of me in that bit of a place, that was built, so they say, when folks mustn't have run as large as now."

This was Reuben Ken's ecclesiastical situation, set before him in a way that, to him, did not seem to lighten what would be his labours in the future.

It was clear enough to him, that it would be nothing short of a mockery to go about bidding all come, when only about a fourth of the least grown could sit or stand. And, like the better part of the Anglican clergy, who feel that whilst they have not room for all, they have not a clear conscience before God, Reuben Ken bethought himself how he could best occupy a place, that was built for two hundred, with six hundred more.

He laid awake a good many nights thinking if he dared to build; and one night he thought he dared. The next morning he began to put his thoughts together.

together. To open a subscription for more church room wanted, perhaps, a good deal of hard faith in an outlying district, where God's name was taken in vain if ever it was taken at all.

There was only one big house that could be said to be good for anything, and that was the Hall; but it was not to let just then. There was the property of Mr. Richard Ken—Mr. Richard Ken never gave to churches—and when his son was moved to go into the church, Mr. Richard Ken did give up his pew. It was his belief that more colds were caught in a church than "on 'change." Mr. Ken thought God might very well be worshipped without sitting in a thorough draught; nor was that gentleman at all above being profane in his much humour. "If that was God's house," he he said one cool forenoon "on 'Change," "it must be His summer house," and the pleasantry was for a season freely quoted in the circles which he leavened.

It was quite Reuben Ken's first experience, that to make a big church out of a little one,

one, on the contingency of filling it, is a thing to be begun in a man's morning of life, if it is ever to be done at all.

Monies, however, such as they were, did come in. A special sermon produced in the morning and evening thirteen shillings and fourpence ; which gross offering would have been attributed to a fit of unprofessional absence on the part of an attorney, who happened to be " doing " those parts, with a change of clothes in a blue bag, but that the contribution was made wholly up of copper.

Six weeks gave a hopeful total of between two and three pounds that had been hard enough to get ; but these were evidences that the district had been bled for church purposes as much as was safe.

Reuben Ken was sorely put to it to know what he should do. Sometimes he thought he had better give the money back. But the sight of the six hundred souls without a church, kept him from going back, and it was in this strait that he sought out Caleb Dane.

It

It was not the first, nor was it the second visit that Reuben Ken had made to the beautiful old cottage-home of Mr. Dane. The district had not a whole doctor to itself. A professional person, of some parts, rode over ten miles twice a week, and he gave another day when there was any epidemic. This gentleman, at such times as he came, was to be seen in the parlour of the best inn for three hours in the middle of the day, between which visitations it was absolute dying to fall sick. Tuesdays and Fridays were the appointed days for getting ill.

Neither was there a lawyer; an indication, it might be, that there was nothing in those parts fit to possess, so that there could be nothing for which it was possible unhappily to strive. It might have been a sign of barbarism, or otherwise, an opinion to be decided only by the various sorts of individual reverence for lawyers.

When Reuben Ken first entered on his cure, a nonconforming pawnbroker, who had no stated charge—although he did not set

set himself against realising what he could,
—was got to give an opinion when any bad
breach of the peace seemed likely.

Mr. Dane, whose family had lived there
for some generations, was very generally
respected. Mr. Dane was not at all respected, as I have heard this said of hard
men with great "balances" in Lombard
Street. He came amongst those who
needed him, when something beyond good
advice was wanted. He did not look on
those about him and some way below him
in what they earned, as mere "hands;"
but he was known as an employer who was
irregular enough, moreover, to think something of the "hands'" souls.

Caleb Dane, however you might put
him out, was not at all the man to let a
quarrel live.

The cone of dung had not been even a
summer day's revenge; that pile of pro-
vocation had long since ceased to give
offence to Richard Ken; and in the hearty
welcome the farmer gave to Reuben, and
to the son of an ill-favoured, ill-conditioned
neighbour,

neighbour, there was not one bitter memory of the past.

It was of this unselfish and large-hearted yeoman, that Reuben Ken in his first trouble came to take some counsel.

It was a beautiful June afternoon when the curate, who, it must be said, did not much like the business he was bent on, made his third visit to the farmer's home, which was, by the chronicles of the neighbourhood,—chronicles, with truth sufficient in them to make them in that seeming rare,—not much younger than the church.

By very credible annals it was in Roman Catholic times, once the priest's house, and to this day retains its title of St. Mona's.

Mr. Dane, who was not nearly an "Evangelical" enough to care for any number of such legends, on his first coming into possession, had been talked to, to no very great purpose, by the dissenters, who came to him in clusters, declaring the name was an abomination. It was even told him, with an air that forbade jesting, that some former travelled Pope,

anxious

anxious to see " the Lakes," had come there in disguise, and had rented the place for weeks, returning to Rome, as it was only likely he should, in the debt of the landlord. But with these, and with other such like terrors, it still remained St. Mona.

Reuben Ken had not been waiting very long, when the farmer entered the best parlour, followed by a beautiful girl.

" Edith, this is Mr. Ken; Mr. Ken, my daughter."

Edith Dane, it may be said at once, was not at all the girl whose image can be told. It may be noted that she was then not quite seventeen; that there was just so much of her as there should be of a woman; that she was neither fair nor dark ; that her eyes were not " fine eyes," but soft, warm, never-to-be-forgotten, balmy eyes. I do not know that her rounded form was perfect. A spare woman, whose authority from her point of view should have its weight, would have called her gross,—and some of the spare women of the district *called* her gross. I do not know that

that her features were perfect; but it was hard to look, with whatever criticism you might, upon the form or face of Edith Dane, girl and woman just then mingling, and feel that anything was wanting. She was a beautiful girl, and that may not to any purpose be figured out in words.

Reuben Ken had not heard a little of the loveliness of Edith Dane. Every one on his coming whom he met, wanted to be the first to tell him what was thought of the little one he had sometimes played with as a boy; and for miles round, and for many of them, Edith's praise was on all lips.

In the autumn months those who came there to climb the hills managed to find some cause for getting to St. Mona; and it was not considered a very great scandal, that Edith drew more of the climbers to church to look at her, than ever any parson had by any sermon.

St. Mona had been her cradle. She had never left it for the refined pollution of a school. Imaged like her mother, to her father she supplied a void, and was his all

in

in all. Edith was like her mother, and got more like as time went on.

Around the memory of the idol that was gone, the heart of Caleb Dane had told him that he could not love again. But the form and face of the dead seemed like a resurrection in the living; and whilst he knew it not, he had yet raised up a second idol in his child.

Edith, since her mother's death, had been chiefly educated by an aunt, a woman of great discipline of life, herself of excellent intentions, and with all the acknowledged purposes about her of strict " Evangelical Protestantism."

Edith, when not yet seventeen, had come back to her father,— her aunt would have it in a series of letters she wrote upon the calamity of an undeveloped education, full three years too soon.

Reuben Ken soon got to know that the enlargement of his church to the desired size would not at all alienate him from the society of Miss Dane. The society of Miss Dane soon became a very material

part

part of the church building scheme. Indeed, as many perpetual curates so situated have before, he soon began to fancy that the one had a great deal to do with the other. Every time he saw Edith, and those times were strangely multiplied, the church in his imaginings greatly grew; after awhile there was all the promise that it was quite likely to be very big.

Notwithstanding what her excellent aunt had said about the evil of young High Church clergymen always wanting to build, Edith saw the state of things that was to be, very much in the same light as the perpetual curate; and Edith could get together somehow more in a day than could Reuben in a month.

There was none of the counterfeit enthusiasm about the beautiful child of Caleb Dane that so nearly unsexes so very many women. The earnestness that was in her, so feminine, and yet so fitting everything she did, could never be reproached as what is called "demonstrativeness." Her heart was set on that church holding all the souls she pleased,

pleased, but it was not of the frothy nature of that mere impulsiveness, which leads so many at her age to set their hearts on every sort of fashion or adventure. And Edith would get whatever she had set her heart on, if she went amongst the miners in the earth to get it. Amongst these men Edith was a queen; and when she was once told by her aunt, who thought miners were no company for maidens, that those big men used bad words, she witnessed truly when she said she never heard one.

But with all that could be brought to bear in the summing up, it seemed that twenty pounds was the most which, even by such means as Edith knew, could be got together at St. Hilda's. Still the curate, when he looked at the thing narrowly and closely, could not bring his mind to think the time ill spent; nor, it may be, did Edith of St. Mona either.

When the next summer came round something would be got out of the climbers who came to " do " the mountains and see the view; and perhaps the name
of

of Edith Dane drew quite as many to St. Hilda's as the mountains.

But churches would never grow, and perpetual curates, it is likely, would not always mind if they did not, if they might not nurse a fancy for their very chief lay labourer.

Mr. Dane, who had heard of the church building, as a symptom of what was coming, saw what now had come, and perhaps he did not stay it. Reuben felt it, and he did not chill it ; but Edith only saw what must be, unsuspectingly.

" I'm afraid we shall never succeed, Mr. Ken," said Edith, one afternoon, adding up a stubborn total of nineteen pounds nineteen shillings and ninepence. " We are still threepence off the twenty pounds ; but the church ought to be bigger, although aunt says there are too many churches, and not enough chapels. I don't think so, and I am sure something ought to be done for your house, Mr. Ken ; it is not fit to live in."

"Could you not then live there, Edith ?"— Edith !

Edith! It was the first time he had ever taken that name on his lips before her. Often had he spoken it in his prayers; often had he shouted it, in a rambling way, upon the mountain side, but never till that day before her.

"I have never thought if I could live there; but why do you ask, Mr. Ken?" said Edith, with that unaffected innocence which would pass for boldness in a London drawing-room, or at a very finishing school.

"Because I am going to ask you, Edith, if you will let me, to live there with me always."

"Reuben!"

"Yes; there, Edith — as my wife."

"But that won't make the church get bigger, will it? and that's what you came to talk about this afternoon," said Edith, whose warm smile told Reuben that where he could live, she felt that perhaps she might; and that afternoon—for in such matters it is not well to lose much time— instead of at all seeking the threepence that should have made the twenty pounds, the

two

two fresh hearts, that never could be twain again, laid their burden before Mr. Dane.

Mr. Dane, who struggled to look firm, said all that on such an occasion might be said.

He was quite sure that Reuben was not well old enough to marry, and that Edith was much too young; but in his heart the farmer said, " I will not part them longer than the winter;" and when the winter came round, Reuben thought he should write to his father to tell him of his coming marriage ; and his father, who had once said in a fatherly way, " Never let me hear of you again," wrote back to heap fresh city curses on his son. The language of the moneyed man was even foul; a great way worse than ever. But Reuben Ken, who had known he would be cursed afresh, on Christmas Eve took Edith Dane to his own home; and on his wedding-day received from Mr. Dane one thousand pounds, and the bit of freehold, that had been for many years between those families a " raw."

And there was no measure to their love ;

their

their world lay in that little home. To the one, the care unuttered, was lost in the sympathy that was felt to be supreme. That sympathy which might cast out fear for what could ever be.

Oh! days, hours, minutes, what will be their measure, what their span, in the balance of the agonies that shall fret the coil you yet shall step on? Atoms as they shall be, when you take their reckoning in the past, hold them when you can; believe in them, before your shrivelling faith shall see in every loveliness a lie. And when it seems you can, take thought that what you grasp, or better said, that what you *think* you grasp, has no more substance than the pictures of sleep, or the night mists of summer. And when it seems you can, the " when " shall be the " lie," its mockery the " life."— " Ever " shall be the dream—the waking " never."

CHAP.

CHAP. V.

Of the First Concession.—Of the Failing Crumb.

REUBEN KEN had sufficient cause to have some time learnt, that all within his cure were not of one way of thinking. St. Hilda's being a preferment very little worth the holding—if worth holding at all—although many of its perpetual curates had gone to their rest with their minds made up about it—it had been held, a great way beyond the memory of any one then living, by tolerable men of only a very lax conformity. They were of sober life, with the necessary aggregate of its decent observances; always with large families, which had never done increasing; generally with twins;

F 3 sometimes

sometimes with thirteen plain girls ; and with what they believed to be a judicious liking for the " Record," any number of weeks after publication.

It was not remarkable that church principles should not take much under their preferment. It was remarkable that they should take anything. It was nothing to them that episcopacy should continue ; but it was everything to them that their preferment should not cease. The difference between the ministry, and the meeting house to them was, that they took their sixty pounds a year, after some sort of certainty. It was not strange that they should be taken very generally for what they seemed ; and the nonconformists of St. Hilda's, who rather overran it, were abundantly satisfied that nonconformity, under a rule so little divided, would take no very great hurt.

This was a negative way of looking at the callousness of the curates, which hardly represented the real satisfaction of schism. Dissent could take no ill whilst the perpetual

petual curates were of such a sort. There
was nothing in the calvinism of the whole
succession of ministers, from which it had
been possible to dissent. These were no
" prayer-book clergymen." The conventicle had become the church, and the church
was the conventicle.

Reuben Ken's immediate predecessor—
a man who had some very emphatic fancies
of his own for what he called "the revision
of the liturgy," and would, perhaps, have
improved it from the service altogether—
had, on one Monday morning, so it was
given out, forgotten to send his one surplice to the wash; but nonconformity, if
just then without occupation, was still
there to applaud, and to superintend.

It was very delicately represented, that it
would make one fold of the place, if the
surplice never went to the wash again.
There was thought to be a good deal in
this, and the " soiled superstition," as the
vestment was christened, was put away.

Conformity at St. Hilda's was after this
sort, and about at this ebb, when the pre-

ferment,

ferment, after being almost hopelessly re-
fused, passed into the hands of Reuben
Ken.

Of church feeling there was none ; no
one knew what it meant ; and what little
public prayer there was, seemed the monopoly of schism.

The " dissenting divines" were the ministers of accident.   There was, a great way
before anybody else, a preaching pawnbroker, who had acquired his brilliant delivery over his duplicates ; and others there
were any length behind, tiring to get near
him, and catch whatever might be of his
inspiration ; but the protestantism of St.
Hilda's, it was easy to see, was in the hands
and mouth of the pawnbroker.

This gentleman attended in an official
sort of way, the first Sunday of Reuben's
coming, to listen to the reading in, and
hear the sermon.   Everything, it had
transpired in some circles, would depend
on what took place.   The chapel, which
had pipes all over it, could be warmed in

an

an hour, so "Protestant" worship would be secured.

Reuben Ken, who had only come late on the Friday night, had heard nothing of the "evangelical" church discipline which had bound his predecessors. Some one set to watch had seen what was taken to be a surplice between the church and the Parsonage ; and report in every way confirmed that the curate, even in those early days, had asked if there was an organ.

Now, if anything to some people is the chief toy of "Anti-Christ," it is an organ. The pawnbroker when he heard it cleared his throat,—not at all to sing,—that throat on which any organ was an imputation ; and it was gathered from his symptoms, that he thought Protestantism would be likely to take hurt.

Reuben Ken was perfectly satisfied when, he looked around upon the congregation, that had come to hear him the first morning. There was not an empty seat. It came over him, as he looked on that gathering, that it should be the busy work of his

life,

life, the work in which he would never tire, to keep those seats there full. But he was very new indeed to that of which he never meant to tire; and it did not even exceptionally enter into his calculations, the sort of work that there would be.

His was beyond question a church-going cure. When he came to the first lesson he had begun to think that this was perhaps why it was only sixty pounds a year. The worship was very essentially congregational, even if a very little harsh. The clerk was perhaps overpowered by the pawnbroker's immense capacity for continuous response; but that person was clearly an unsalaried duplicate of the parish stipendiary.

Reuben Ken might have seen that the organ spoke, as though it had been some time without speaking, and that the mind of the congregation was clearly set against the instrument returning to so bad a habit. So far, a good deal answered the worst expectations of the pawnbroker. Everything would hang about the sermon. That would

would open the chapel, or keep its doors
closed. Of all this, it had been taken care,
that Reuben Ken should know nothing.
He remembered indeed to have sate out
some services there with his mother when
a boy, but of the ecclesiastical sensitive-
ness of St. Hilda's he had everything
to learn. What he should wear would
decide a good deal. If he wore nothing
outside his coat in the pulpit, the pawnbroker might be got to stay with the fold.
But Reuben Ken mounted the pulpit stairs
in his surplice. The crisis had come. Anyone in white in that pulpit had never been
seen before; but as there was no vestry
there was still the chance, till Reuben
had given out the text, that he would yet
strip it off and cast it from him. But
when Reuben Ken preached there, without any excuse for the white thing he stood
in, for twenty minutes, and addressed them,
chiefly concerning the end of his own
coming amongst them, and the authority
of the church to set him over them, and
although never perhaps was that authority

more

more tenderly and less dogmatically proclaimed, yet, taken with the unaccountable
revival of the organ, and the apparelling of
his person in a surplice, an offence had
clearly been conveyed, which, it was very
necessary to meet at once, and which could
be only met in one fashion.

It was, in a measure, comforting to the
critics who had come so far to cavil, when
the pawnbroker turned himself about as
the surplice innovation had become confirmed, and nodded in a manner which
could not be mistaken, and which brought
assurance. The congregation felt that a
crisis was imminent, and were very glad
that it should be, as they gathered in groups,
to see what would come of it, in the church
yard.

Suspense, when so much was at stake,
would have been too much for schism; and
it was very soon clear that, the pawnbroker
had something to say, which would indi-
cate the course of action, and he mounted,
and clung to a gravestone to say it.

There was not, perhaps, so much expressed.

pressed. Empires have been saved by a
syllable, and churches by a word; but
whilst a chapel in this instance was to be
declared open by a sentence, the severest
commentary on Mr. Ken's proceedings was
understood, when the pawnbroker gave
out, as Reuben passed, that there would be
"*Protestant* worship in the chapel that
same afternoon at three o'clock." And
there was. And Mr. Ken was prayed for
and against, by a chapel full; for, that he
might see his peril and be brought to
Protestantism; against, that he and all
such, might be cast out of the fold, by some
spirited process not just then determined
on; and in this special praying everything
appearing in white, and all organs came to
be included.

Later in that day, Mr. Ken's belief, in
the liking of his parish for its church, un-
derwent some change. There was not so
much as a congregation of twelve at church
in the afternoon. Perhaps his people dined
early and were heavy; but even he began
to suspect that their staying away was
hardly

hardly to be traced to their general over-eating. Something, it was clear, had divided the flock; and Reuben Ken was told in the evening what he had done.

The clerk, who was a man of few words, did not seem disposed to tell a great deal; so Mr. Ken asked him to supper, and during the meal, under some little pressure, the cause of offence came out.

Reuben Ken would have conceded anything for "peace." He thought much more highly of peace, than of principles. He could understand people dying for peace, but he could not at all understand that any one could be burnt for principles. He respected orthodoxy, but he liked to get it without discussion. He liked things decently done. He had not an irreverential mind, but he did not know—and he would much rather not know—when to relax and when to be firm. Reuben Ken in this matter has so many imitators, that it is not hard to understand how he was always giving in, when he should have been the rather holding out. He thought very well

on

on the whole of the Articles, but he had subscribed to them chiefly as a matter of peace.
If the Liturgy was in any manner hateful
to those without the church, it was as well,
he thought, that they should be conciliated.
No one could ever tell where the churchmanship of Reuben Ken ended or began.
He would have resigned his cure to have
escaped controversy.

Since the ministry of Reuben Ken, the
ordinances of the church—as the present
age abundantly evidences—have so come to
be lightly regarded, and unfaithfully minis-
tered by, an unsatisfied and undistinguished
section of the clergy, who seek to set up their
conscience as the excuse for their cavilling.
This miserable latitudinarianism, whilst it
hinders and scandalises the Establishment,
does not lessen schism. The spirit of concession only just stops short—if it does stop
there—of a virtual surrender of the Liturgy; and whilst it so stops short, it is
concession thrown away.

It was so with Reuben Ken; and to get
back his congregation, who would not sit
out

out the service that he was set over them to administer, he was prepared to surrender everything that could give effect to his authority. The dissenters, as is not exceptional, accepted his concession, but they did not close their chapel.

" You see, it's the organ a playing again of a sudden that they couldn't bear; and that white gown," said the clerk, " the gennelman afore you never thought the more than nothing, of wearing anything upon him but his coat, and put a stop to the organ."

" But, my good friend, I don't insist upon an organ; pray, can't this be understood? I'm for peace, where it's possible. I don't think much of a surplice, though I can't preach in my coat. It wouldn't do; I should be certainly admonished by my bishop."

" That's where it is you've gone and hit it; directly you begin in this place to talk of bishops, and them sort of people, it's all up with you. A bishop ain't of no account here; it isn't worth thinking about;

about; for the gennelman who was here
afore you gave up everything clean, so that
there wasn't nothing left, and then they
wasn't pleased."

"But," continued Reuben, casting about
to see how much more he might give
away to keep the peace, "I could have
congregational singing to be sure, which,
after all, is perhaps the simplest; and I
will preach in a black gown. I particularly
wish to avoid giving offence by any prejudices — by any extremes. Who is this
preacher at the chapel? if he would come
over and see me, I feel that these differences
would cease, and that I could at least assure him."

"You be like all the rest of 'em as ever
came here," said the clerk. "It's no use
giving way, and I told 'em so; and it's less
use now than ever it was. No one after a
bit, will see what's the difference between
you and him. If it's the pawnbroker that
you be meaning, and wanting to see, it ain't
quite likely that he'll come to you; he
doesn't reckon that you're as good as him,
and

and I don't know that he'd see you for certain if you went to him."

These were some of the prospects of his parish that opened up to the perpetual curate of St. Hilda's the great, the first Sunday that he came amongst his people; and in the next six weeks every concession that he could offer was put into the scale, but they went for nothing. It only ended in the chapel pipes being looked to; the efforts he subsequently made to enlarge the church were accepted only as a challenge to the work of the dissenters; and it would have been quite sufficiently hard to say, in what the conventicle differed from the church, or the church from the conventicle.

And after this and a worse sort, was the struggle which the perpetual curate had, by his own weakness, brought to some strength, when Reuben married Edith Dane; and as he took her home, he could only hopelessly talk to her of what he had conceded, in what he had not gained.

Edith

Edith had seen through her husband's want of purpose, in some measure before they were married; and she now comprehended it entirely, when one morning after listening to what he had to say, and hearing him blame every cause but the right one, she hinted, whether he were not perhaps assimilating his own services, a great way too nearly to those of the nonconformists, and to such lengths, that, it was not easy for a parish easily confused, to say whether, the church or the chapel was the least likeness of the Establishment.

But Reuben Ken, even with his wife's words to rally him, was not to be got to see anything in such a light. He had seen everything so much the other way that he did not take at all to the new view. He had not liked shutting up the organ, and being driven to preach in a black gown, and apologising in many different forms for the authority of his own office. But he had actively begun at the wrong end; he meant to carry this end right through, believing it to be the right one.

He

He had conceded everything, and in the adding up it came to him that he had carried nothing.

The perpetual curacy of St. Hilda's, as a preferment, was, either a toy for a man who might be already beneficed over much, or a spare, and a bare living at the best, to those, who had in some earnest, to look to the living, for what they and theirs should take to eat. Indeed the state of things was a very regular one. St. Hilda's had been variably held by a pluralist, and by a pauper.

Neither Reuben Ken nor his wife found that sixty pounds a year went very far. Edith, indeed, had pretty much the measure of their means. She knew how many days in the week she dared to set a piece of gravy meat upon the table, and how many days she did not dare to set it there; but there are times, even as the wives of clergymen so beneficed must know, when contriving itself becomes demoralised and out of sorts, and even the candle ends have not another end to serve.

As

As getting the church to a more likely
size, had first brought Reuben and his wife
together, how to bring its greater size
about, with such a nonconforming element
against them, was the first difficulty that
they brought their blended life to face.
They had faith that there would be bread
to fill any number of mouths; but their
faith was nothing like so large in church
extension.

Mr. Dane had dowered his daughter
with a thousand pounds, which was not
an indifferent sum to put by; and it was
worth so much the more because it was
theirs to do what they would with it; and
what they would do with it, was to give it
to the church. If Mr. Dane could have
seen this very decent sum dropped over
their Utopian plan of free seats, he would
have tied it up a good deal tighter. They
thought then, that something could be
done on sixty pounds a year; and that to
sink a thousand pounds under a church,
was getting rid of a responsibility to themselves,

selves, in a manner that would save some souls.

A gentleman, who had testimonials from Mr. Pugin, was commissioned to do what he thought would be best with the thousand pounds; and what that gentleman, by what he did, thought best, was seemingly a very little, for a good moiety of the six hundred bodies could never any the more get inside. Had Mr. Dane survived, the little church would have remained little; but he died suddenly in the early spring; and when they had buried him away, Reuben and his wife hardly dared remind each other, that they were left to face the world alone, on sixty pounds a year.

It will never be told that they ever came to be worse than they were. What they passed through, will be written as their record—written as those thin fingers left it. If it may seem too hard to have belonged to their being, it is a bit of the book of their lives.

Their first born came upon St. Crispin's day.

day. And whether it was, because, as Edith
said, when she was minded of a week's
account, that in those early days was
hard to meet, her third cousin, once removed, who was called Crispin, might do
something for them—whether it was after
the third cousin, once removed, or whether
it was after the saint, the boy was christened Crispin.

This third cousin once removed heard
of the way he had been thought of, over
the font, with very remarkable emotion;
and he knew, or he thought he knew—and
it was the only side of nature which in the
counting-house he had ever known—that
taking the name given to him at his baptism, was meant to be a moral lien upon as
much of his undisposed of property as might
be. The way he did business himself, and
the great ends that came of it, made it very
necessary that he should be everlastingly
suspicious; so he sent for his solicitor, and
strengthened the approaches to his property accordingly. It was very horrible
for him to think that anybody with his
name

name would ever come to him to ask for
anything that he had left upon his plate
to eat; and it was likely that this was all
that would ever come of the compliment.
A man, he thought, who with sixty pounds
a year, could sink a whole thousand pounds
under a church, would never have the sink-
ing of a groat of his. He reserved his respect for only those, who could show by
large evidences, that they knew the value of
money.

Within the first ten years of their married life three children were born to them.
When the first had come, there were ugly
seemings that there was quite enough, for
another sixty pounds a year to do. But
Reuben Ken, thought only of the blessing
that was on his home, when Edith called
on him to love a daughter; for before all,
in' that little one the mother spoke; and
she was christened Mona. The third gave
a brother to Crispin, and him they called
John.

But little Jack, by which name he soon
came to be the better known, was lame,
and

and lame it was said—unless by a miracle,
which the doctor did not apprehend would
ever be worked in such a place as St.
Hilda's—he would be so long as he lived;
and it might be, it was told, that he would
grow less comely, if he grew at all, every
day till he was laid down to die.

And in these times, what the sixty
pounds a year could do, grew less. But
Edith's heart, was set on keeping the hard
knowledge of this back from Reuben; and
how she did it, only the wife who has stood
where she stood, can come out from her own
life's labour, and can tell. But it well may
be, that the agony, which has never seemed
to suffer, whilst the smile has beamed its
ever love, as the coverlet must go to get a
crust, has never yet been told. The cry
for bread rung in her ears, and she must
find the bread, and not let ever so little of
the cry ring in *his* ear. She cannot say to
him that they have come to be short of
bread; she cannot say to *them*, as they follow her from emptiness to emptiness, and
hang to her thin dress, that their cry, the

cry

cry of the flesh and blood of a clergyman, is short of reason. This, where an appearance must be kept, and bread must be got, is where woman is the chiefest hope of home; where hunger stands by the hearth side, and those there withering up, have learned where hope may end. The cry of the least of her little ones, has driven her to the locker that she knows to be a void. She hears the father promise bread. She hears the footfall of the youngest nearing her to get its crust; and when its little head is on her breast, she must stay that weakening cry; but it shall be suffered her that time to save; and she shall know how nearly by too much, a bit of bread was quite beyond their reach.

Through years, Edith Ken had been so tried. The whole house would look to her. Sixty pounds a year, when times are at their best, does not contemplate a servant, even of all work. A servant would have liked, as little as might be, the fare on which it was perhaps a marvel that they did not die; and without, and beyond, the decencies of clerical life,—for the sake of

of the church,—had to be preserved. The
church gave sixty pounds a year, and so of
course expected it. You cannot, however
you may set about it, get a mixed population, to think well all round of a clergyman, who has butcher's meat just once a
week, and says a special grace for that.
Considerations in the main, not absolutely
favourable to church principles, will come
up; and the sensualist, who likes everything
comfortable, and well ground down to the
corner, of what he believes to be the religion
to which he clings, thinks it ever so great,
a pity that, clergymen do not do such
things, as will enable them to get a bit of
meat at less rare intervals.

For the first ten years of the hard struggle,
that was ever getting harder, very little of
the curate's need was known beyond his
door. Indeed, with Edith there, and with
her many ways of keeping back the worst,
he had not felt the keenest of their wants
himself. When *he* was called to eat, the
loaf was whole. He had never seen the
last crust hidden in a corner; and what

with

with his parish, which he worked well meaningly, whilst he was ever thinking out some fresh concession ; and his two boys who did not look so sickly, though they had been sparely fed, Reuben Ken, as should every parish priest, refrained himself from taking pupils.

About this time he seems to have begun an unconnected diary, and to have continued it at varying intervals over many years. At one place it is written :

" *Dec. 4th.*—This day I have had to pay the doctor's bill, which seemed a long one ; but I may not think so, for we have all been sick at times of late. He has dealt fairly with me, and it is for two years' watchfulness of Jack, whose leg I fear the rather shortens. I must give up something to pay this doctor's bill. I have told Edith she must stay all butcher's meat for a short season. She says we shall do well ; but I do not know how we can do much worse. I would not tell her this, but I must be for weeks without a shilling in the house."

" *Jan.*

"*Jan.* 1*st*.--I have parted with a little furniture this new year's day; we have not now a chair a piece; but Edith says we can yet awhile keep all the beds, for which I am thankful. I hope my people will not get to hear of this, as they may think the less well of my ministry."

"*June* 3*rd*.--I have much sorrow that Jack, who is my chief grief, can no longer get his left leg to the ground. I am told that I should give him as much port wine as he can drink, and that nothing else can serve him. Then his little foot must go on shrinking, and I must give back my boy. This night I have not a shilling to buy bread."

"*Nov.* 4*th*.--My wife has got a chill; she will not tell me how bad it is, so I am forced to guess; but she says her cough is nothing. It has been nothing, I fear to think, too long. It has been a great time with her, and she seems to waste."

"*Dec.* 1*st*.--I am sick myself to-day. I can only just crawl about the room, and

am

am very weak. I do not complain; for up till now, God has always given me my health. Edith says that she is better; but the doctor does not say so much about it.

"Two of the bedsteads went to-day to get Edith blankets. I pray God that I may always bear His will. There is no bread for to-morrow. Jack's clothes are past mending, and Mona cannot work as once."

"*Dec. 20th.*—This day has my cow been seized, and the sow will go to-morrow. We are in a great strait. Mona has her mother's cough. Jack is now so nearly naked, that he cannot go decently abroad. Crispin is a great comfort to me, but I wish he took more kindly to concession. We have fasted these last twelve hours through. We want food sorely, every one. I pray God I may not come to beg; but I do not know how we shall face the morrow; for He does not give us now our daily bread."

CHAP.

CHAP. VI.

The Grave in the Sand.

THERE is a great, and what may be a meaning, gap in the diary of Reuben Ken after the day the sow was seized; so for a while there is no record how they got, or went without, their daily bread.

It may indeed be better said there are all the means of believing, that for a while they got none; but then better things it seems had come upon them, and these better things for a little while had seemed to stay.

Some one with a herd of beasts gave them a dun cow, that there were, it was believed, very sufficient reasons for believing, would never at the best of times yield a

G 4

quart

quart of milk again. But these veterinary and friendly calculations, were in the end at fault, and so it turned out that no dry beast was the gift cow.

It was nearly twenty years since the day Reuben Ken had read himself in at the little church of St. Hilda's the great — since ever the organ had been heard to speak,—since he had unwittingly aired, what he dared to call, the authority of his office in a surplice,—and the pawnbroker, who had been the while moving on to his meridian as a minister, was still the better man.

Reuben Ken, in those twenty years, had gone through a great deal, and had every year found out the more, that sixty pounds was less than he could live on. When he had not suffered as much, as most about him did, it was only when he had suffered more.

No one could say that the conscience of the perpetual curate was ever, at the hardest times, far away from what he did. He gave more than a little of all the little that he had; and when his weaknesses are forgotten,

gotten, and he has been laid away, there shall steal back a genial memory of what he did, with what he had, that even here, where there is no stone above him, shall speak over his dust, better than though it spoke in marble. For other than this, there shall be no big stone. But the little ones, on whom he ever gently laid his hand, and blessed them as he passed along,—too often empty returning to his emptiness at home —shall cease their play over his head, where the grass grows green, and hold their breath, —when they think of the things, that tell of what he did, to those who came before them—and not play out their marbles there.

Reuben Ken had only made up his full mind to this one thing; he only knew that he wanted peace. " If," as he would say — struggling for union, and getting the while the further from it—" the dissenters do not like a surplice, why should I wear one when I preach ?" and he reasoned within himself that there was a good deal in this, so he put away the white for the black ; but the dissenters, who neither

liked

liked the signs of white nor black, did not
somehow turn to fill his church.

There are a great many Reuben Kens,
without his heart or his simplicity—not
only in proprietary chapels and " Evangelical" preferments—on whom the laying on
of hands has not been well; with all the
weaknesses of the curate of St. Hilda's,
and yet without his lively meaning to keep
straight.

Reuben Ken, it is here protested, must
not be written down—or written up it
perhaps should be,—an " Evangelical."

If he had been set down for life where
nonconformity had a lesser hold, Reuben
Ken would have put out the colours of
a churchman. He liked things decently
done. He saw the ritual betrayed, with a
good deal of applause about the betrayal,
at the hands of hundreds eating the bread
of the church, and carrying that bread
about in sheets of the " Record."

Reuben Ken thought the betrayal grievous enough ; but he did not see in how
much he was betraying it himself.

                                        It

It was quite the same with his schools,
if not after a sort, perhaps a little worse.
The pawnbroker had been zealous to pack
a committee. Mr. Ken might well have
been too much for the packing, have ral-
lied the churchmen, and have said a good
deal to the purpose about the church holding her own; but this seemed to him of
all things, just another great occasion for
concession.

If the dissenters were anxious to join
churchmen on their own ground, he thought
it would be well to go out to meet them.
If they wanted, as it seemed they did, to
help to sow the good seed in the virgin
soil, should their zeal, he asked, be made a
reproach to them? It is not easy for those
who look on and give judgment now, to
understand at all, why any perpetual curate
should have been so largely fooled, and why
he did not see, what so irresistibly brought
the dissenters, to have a little digging in
the virgin soil.

So the virgin soil was, as soon as might
be, a dirt where nothing orthodox would

ever

ever grow; and the concession, whilst it went to paralyse the hands of the church, did not conciliate any one dissenter.

There were large openings, and the dissenters trooping up crept in, and thereout they took nothing to their own advantage that was very small.

It was the same with the book club, and the parish reading-room. The pawnbroker, who was as ever, too much for the perpetual curate, after having got divers prints of his own sort, played a great game; and the great game that the pawnbroker played took this sort of line. With an air amounting to benevolence, he proposed the "Record" as a genial thing for "church" reading. Reuben Ken, who on sixty pounds a year had never given any part of it to a church newspaper, did not at all know how far the "Record" might exhaust church sympathies; but the pawnbroker's offer was too much for the curate. It spoke, said Reuben Ken, a great deal for the liberality of a differing brother, and perhaps too, it said something for the "Record."

But

But the kindliness of Reuben Ken had
in those twenty years got for him, as well
it might, a friend or two without his parish;
and *in* his parish, others would have grouped
themselves about him, long before the
twenty years had been but ten, had it been
evidenced, however little, that he knew
anything of the philosophy of not giving
up a point, when so much depended on
holding the point the tightest.

Reuben Ken had been in the class list
himself; and at nineteen it was believed
that Crispin, if he could have the opportunity, was quite likely to do even better
things, even in the same way.

And he had the luck to have his chance
of getting to those better things.

A neighbouring squire, whose heart kept
company with his purse — nor could the
one at any time reproach the other — and
perhaps had a tendency to plethora, managed, as with such it is not hard to manage,
without letting Reuben Ken know why
or how he did it, to introduce himself to
Crispin, and in the end to set him over
his

his two sons ; and this was done as decently as such things can be, when the offer does not seem to tell the offered of his little means.

The squire indeed had come to hear—and perhaps it might be, that all his life through he had laid himself out for hearing just such things—how the sow went, and how the cow was fetched away, years after they had suffered, as security; and he took occasion to ask the curate to dinner in a friendly way.

A dinner in " a friendly way " may mean a table on which there is but little set, and an apology or two for setting out so little, whilst it was never meant to set out more ; but this was not that squire's friendly sort of dinner.

The curate had not dined away from home—he and his children reckoned up—for fifteen years; and it was quite the work of a week to get him fit, and Reuben Ken was never very fit, even after all was done ; but Edith, who had sewed up his clothes, and nearly conquered every breaking out, said

said " he would do ;" and perhaps this was
the more sure to her, because her husband
wore her father's cast-off coat.

After dinner, the squire found the way
to make the curate drink a good deal of
dry wine.

The squire kept filling the curate's glass,
till the curate seemed to think that many
things were multiplied about him. But
nothing set aside the thought, that this
was the wine the doctor said which Edith
ought to drink ; and in the end he did not
greatly wonder at the doctor's faith in it.

The squire drew up his legs, and got
himself well together in his great arm-
chair, and, holding his glass up to the
light, said, "It's a pleasant wine, Mr. Ken,
though I say it ; it hasn't lost its body.
What do you think of it ? It was bottled
in '14. Nothing of the cork about it, eh ?
and it keeps its colour wonderfully. That
green seal made the fortune of two generations."

" It's very fine, remarkably fine," said
the curate, wondering how much a little
seal

seal in green could do; "and it doesn't
seem to have lost its body. Perhaps it is
a little strong, but I do not wonder that
the doctor recommends it. My medical
man, says nothing but this port wine can
get back Edith's—that is, my wife's—
tone."

"God bless you, my dear sir, this isn't
what the doctors send the women; they
don't put this seal to a lady's wine," said
the squire, who began to think that some
of his '48 full flavoured would be good
enough for his guest. "Have you tasted
port like that these twenty years? don't
you feel that it gets hold of you? did you
ever see such a crust? There, sir; I
wouldn't take ten pounds a dozen."

Reuben Ken, who had been reduced to
a good many crusts, with a very good
conscience could remember nothing of the
kind for twenty years; and as he sat there
wondering that there should be a crust in
his glass which he could not see, he had
some time believed, that it must have got
hold of him, even as his host described.

Within

Within a week, a dozen of the green seal came to the curate's wife, with the squire's compliments—the squire fearing it would be shaken to death.

"Take another glass, my friend, it won't hurt you," said the curate's new neighbour; but the curate, who had been seeing a duplicate squire this long time, and more green seals than one, was not to be over persuaded.

"Well, well, do as you like, but I want to have just a word with you about that eldest lad of yours. What do you mean to do with him?"

This was a hard thing for Reuben Ken to answer there and then; it had been some time well to have thought of this, for Crispin had left the lad behind him a good way. He was too old for the sea; besides he couldn't climb; and besides, his mother then never could have borne to have heard the wind at night.

It had been thought of binding him to an attorney, who had woke up one morning, and had bethought himself to take
Crispin

Crispin Ken to do his dirty work—the
proper regular dirty work—for nothing;
but before nightfall, the attorney had calculated, that such a lift in life was clearly
above being given away. So Crispin Ken
was delivered from the law.

It was just then, after the failure of the
attorney's benevolence, one of the curate's
chiefest cares, what he should do with
Crispin.

"Indeed I have not thought. I must
see what I can best afford."

"That's wrong," said the squire, "never
think of a stint over a start; send him to
Oxford, and make a gentleman of him."

There was no doubt about this being
quite the right thing to do. The curate
winced, and the squire went on.

"I shall send him there myself, if you
don't. It's a pity to see such a great lad,
and such a likely lad, milking that cow of,
yours, Mr. Ken."

The curate found it very hard to sit up
there. Whether it was the red wine get-
ing a further hold he did not know, but so

far

far as he knew anything of what was going on, the squire seemed to him to be talking strangely.

"My good friend," said Reuben, as what the squire meant began to dawn, "God knows that I would thank you, but I cannot—cannot."

"And what right have you to say anything about it? I shan't let that great lad milk your cow — don't stop me — you're putting it all out of my head. I know you can't send the boy to Oxford. I know it isn't your fault: some day some people will have a great deal to say about a curate getting less than a butler who is at all particular; but you are all alike; it's just the same with every one of you poor devils; you can't help yourselves, and won't let others help you. There's no need for any explanation. I shall send that lad of yours to Oxford."

Reuben Ken began to feel that everything about him told its story; it was no good to button up his coat; the cloth was much too sensitive to stand coercion.
Nothing

Nothing could get his trousers down where they should be, shake them as he might, whilst both his boots let in the rain. It was no good to try to set aside what he was; he was at best a very ragged man. He could see the squire looking at his coat, and at his waistcoat, which had been made two decades ago for a much larger man; and hardly knowing where he was, or what he said, or what he did, he tried to thank the squire, and then, which was perhaps as hard, he tried to go.

"I tell you, you shall have another glass before you leave this room. I see what it is; you're afraid of it; you've got into your head that it's the doctor's wine. It won't hurt you, man," and the squire poured out another bumper of the ancient wine.

Reuben Ken had the while escaped into the hall for his hat and coat; for he did not know what he might say with more of that wine in him; but the squire was jealous for the '14 port; and Reuben Ken,

Ken, who always liked concession, for peace, was forced to drink it.

"Don't you forget about that lad of yours, Mr. Ken ; and I don't think by the look of him, that he ought to milk your cow much longer."

When the curate had fairly got away, and had told them all at home as well as he could,—and it came out by odd bits at a time, — something about Oxford, and '14, and green seals, and what the squire had it in his head to do for Crispin, so oddly did the curate talk, that no one, when he reached the climax, much believed him.

But when the next day came, and over the breakfast table, his story, if not quite so garnished, did not vary, and to make it surer, a message came down from the squire for Crispin Ken, with a note, something about large lads being fit for better things than milking cows, and a cheque with which to go to Oxford, when he would, it seemed as though they were out of those times which were so hard to bear, and

and that that time had come, when they should sorrow, after no sort, as they had.

"We will have a bit of meat on Sunday," said Edith; "won't it be nice?" and it might have seemed to those who looked upon her, that that bit of meat had only come in time.

"And Mr. Wycherley could come and dine," suggested Mona,

"And we needn't sell the pig," said Jack.

Jack thought that no deliverance could go much beyond the saving of the pigs, for he had petted a lean sow.

But Reuben Ken spoke not at all. His wife stole to his side, and gently there crept up to them both, the other three.

They could not tell how they should keep that day. It was the first time, for more years than any of them could say, that they could dare take thought for the morrow. It was quite a new sensation; and as though the thought in an instant had been born in each, as one, they kneeled down there.

But

But there was a great deal to be done, and a great many to do it, whilst Crispin was yet at his home, and they took their meals more regularly. When one was done, the speculation was less as to when the next should be. The bit of meat was realised; the pigs did not change hands, but got a wash more generous; and, to make it all as well as it could be, Mona's suggestion was considered, and then carried out. Mr. Wycherley was there, and sat next to Mona.

Great things had come to pass, within and without St. Hilda's, the past twelve months, and not the least part was, that there was always something now to eat at the parsonage.

The Rev. John Wycherley had been collated perpetual curate of St. Hilda's the less, a preferment valued roughly at 55*l.* per annum, with certain inexorable outgoings; and where the absence of means in either cure was so definite, the sympathy between the two curates was soon in a measure reciprocal.

Mr.

Mr. Ken had lived on 60*l.* a year for twenty years. He had solved the problem, of how it could be done, as nearly as could be. And so they ate, and they drank together, when between them there had been anything to eat or drink ; and that John Wycherley was often the guest of Reuben Ken, might have had something of a special interest for Mona.

John Wycherley was a man, whose heart and mind, were alike spells to the heart and mind of such a girl as Mona. He was not handsome. He would have been criticised very hardly, had he been called to fill some London pulpits. He was not well looking ; but amidst the minds that chain society, John Wycherley would not have stood unnoticed in a corner. He did not talk at all the average of nonsense, whilst he never set up for a satirist. No one better knew the measure of the hollow world about him. His mind was of a rare order ; and it was of an order, not to be lightly turned in its full force, on any girl so sensitive as Mona ; and to bring them even

even more together, as their sympathies were very much the same, so were their circumstances not unlike.

Mona first began herself to learn, that Wycherley was not indifferent to her, and it may be said, nor she to him, when he was first taught to feel, that it was not so very possible a thing, decently to live on 50*l.*, or thereabouts, a year.

And Mona, fresh and beautiful herself, soon fixed her ideal in John Wycherley; in the man of so much power, committed to so small a sphere. When he came to her feet, with 50*l.* a year to back what he would say, Mona, whose loveliness was known beyond that little cure, might once have married well, very well, the world would say. But the city man, with his thousands, and his thousand friends, looked sickly and yellow in the light of the day; and Mona started from his rhapsodies on gain, and from his parchment skin.

Reuben Ken, who, as any father would, might well have liked to see her better in the world, was very glad when she sent back the rich man; but where she and Wycherley would be, with only 50*l.* a year, was very hard to say.

It was about this time, as near as might be, when it first got about, that the Hall was taken by Ruy Lyle, one of those men, who are looked upon as the agreeable agents of every sort of good, and as powers in what is called, by some miscalling, the " religious world."

But the man, who had bought the Hall, represented this religious world, with some success in his own person. The profane, it was believed, were, in a measure, powerless, so long as he paid his subscriptions; and the " religious world," with instincts gathered from the other world, liked his rich voice, with none the less a fuller liking, because his monies, it was said, could not be told.

Such a man as this, the curate thought, would be, ever so much, too much for the pawnbroker; and, perhaps, just then, when things seemed mending, the curate's only care was for his wife; and Edith, even with the

the '14 port, did not seem to get more strength.

The doctor said, whilst he did not seem to say it hopefully, but only because he must say something, that change of air might work out well, if she was not already too far gone; and an offer made to Reuben Ken about that time, to take some missionary work near Aden, determined him, for a season to leave his cure, in the good hands of Wycherley.

It was to be made worth the curate's while to leave his cure for three years; that is, for the first time since ever he could remember anything, it would be worth his while for what he should get.

With a wife wasting away before his eyes, who never quite ceased by night or day to cough, and whose strength, as it seemed to slip away, must somehow be kept in her; with one boy a cripple, who should have fed more heartily than he could feed, to be got in limb like other men; and with a daughter who must be specially cared for, or go out to take the

H 2   entire

entire charge of other people's children,
and take her share of other people's indifference, — Reuben Ken, at forty-three,
sat down to see how the future could be
met.

There were two hundred pounds a year
tor him, every year he stayed at Aden.
Here was nearly four times as much, as the
cure of souls at home could bring. The
doctor who had gone for change of air, now
saw cause to go against it, and said that
the sand of Aden would be quite the death
of Edith in a month ; but the curate
thought, that he could keep out any sand
with two hundred pounds a year. He
measured what he should do with those
two hundred pounds, by what he had done
upon the sixty, and the measure brought
him the belief, that such a sum could do
most things.

Crispin was to join them from Oxford
as soon as might be ; and the curacy of
St. Hilda's the great, under these circumstances, was so left to the Rev. John
Wycherley, in Reuben's stead.

Everything

Everything seemed new to them on the morning that they went away.

It was the first time they had turned their backs upon their home for twenty years. It had never been expected that the curate's trunks would ever be wanted again, and, but for Jack's great available science in the matter, it was very clear that the boxes, such as they were—for the fashion of boxes even changes many times in twenty years—would never more have left their dust.

But Jack had at no time, very lately, been very long from the cottage of one who has been already heard of in this history, and who was known — and nothing much was known about her — as Mad Meg.

She had come, when Mr. Lyle had come, no one knew how. Those whose business it was to know everything, could not in any manner even tell; but it was said that she kept herself and an idiot child, on the crumbs which fell from the table at the Hall.

H 3   Rumour

Rumour suspected her to have been an old servant of Mr. Lyle's, setting her down as such, a suspicion which the woman herself did not care to say was either false or true; other than this, she seemed to have no history.

Jack Ken took to her at once. He was drawn towards her stricken child, and wherever Mad Meg was, Jack Ken was never far away. Mad Meg's introduction to the curate's family was settled to be very necessary by Jack, and was at once brought properly about by him.

Meg had taken to Jack in her own rough, wild way. She had seen him with her little one about his neck, that little one — the string of whose tongue had never yet been loosed — and between the cripple, and the idiot child, there seemed to be some tightening cord of sympathy that made them one. Meg could see that Jack heard music in the throat that, in its every sound, seemed casting up a taunt at her who bore him. Jack had seen what no one else in St. Hilda's ever had. He had

stood

stood by when Mad Meg cried; and perhaps none other had more cause to know,
how she could either love or hate.

It was Mad Meg who came to get the
curate's trunks to hold together, and when
she had given them as much new life as
they could bear, she asked the curate who
would take his cure.

" Mr. Wycherley, Meg," said Reuben,
" I know you'll all like him."

The curate saw from the sudden change
in the woman's face, unimpressible as she
was, that the coming of John Wycherley,
had its special interest to her.

" I'm sure you'll all be glad to have
him, Meg," said the curate, who, after a
little thinking, fancied this the best way
of finding out Mad Meg's opinion.

But Meg knew what this should mean.
She had had the sort of thing put so to
her, a good many times before. There
was not a little method, in what those who
could not understand her, called her madness; and the absolute vacuity that she

called

called to her face, left the curate as hopelessly unanswered as before.

"Jack," he said aside, "there's something
more in that woman than she cares to tell.
What does Mad Meg know of Mr. Wycherley?"

"Did she tell you she knew anything?"
asked Jack, who saw how Meg would best
like the question answered. But so long
as the curate stayed, whenever John Wycherley happened to be there, Mad Meg
was somehow busy helping in the house.

"He is very kind to her, poor creature,"
said Reuben to himself, still trying to find
out the riddle, as he watched Meg's eyes
ever fixed on Wycherley, as they never
were on any other man or woman. But
he found out nothing, and Wycherley
himself could not take away the puzzle.

Mr. Ken's very moderate expenses were
paid to Aden. The situation was so new
to him, that the instinct of knowing how
to charge was almost dead in him.

It was late in the evening of a hot spring
day,

day, that they came in sight of their new home.

Mr. Ken had meant well all his life. He had meant well, in all the fruitless concessions he had ever made. He had meant well, in angering his father to cut him off. He had meant well, in coming there to live, amidst that ever-thirsty sand, with his hectic wife, who, if she did not die quite soon, could not live long. And, chiefest of all, did Reuben Ken mean well in coming there upon a mission. And in all in which he had ever failed, he had never at all failed like this before.

Some two years after their coming out, Mrs. Ken gave birth to twins. Reuben had a great while thought his quiver to be full enough, but with those twin boys, six pounds a piece in weight, he might speak to some purpose, with any enemy in any gate.

Crispin had joined them just after taking his degree; and as they once more sat around one table, it seemed as though they yet should pass some pleasant weeks together.

It

It was about this time, that Reuben Ken was summoned suddenly many miles away.

Edith lay very feverish and ill, as he passed from the room, where her hot kiss had met his own. He had turned himself about, as we have to do when we pass out into the great jarring world, and leave those we love, perhaps too much, behind. Reuben loved too much ; and the knowledge of it struck him then. The light, from Edith's warm balmy eyes, was turned upon him. It was the last time that he would ever feel the mighty love they spoke.

" Bless you, Edith ! " he said, with the agony of the thought that her call had almost come, " I shall not be long away. I don't think, darling, that your cough is —is—worse."

That cough could not be very easily much worse ; and it was very well for him, he did not see the frothing blood upon the lips which answered him.

She dashed away the crimson witness of her doom—Reuben Ken was gone, and there

there was no meeting here for them
again.

He was about the end of his third day's
journey, when a letter from his home was
put into his hand. It was from his wife,
pencilled in the weakness of the change
that was upon her. She urged him to
come back, and not to stay upon the road,
if he would see her alive.

She had been taken with a fever, and
her little ones had taken it from her.

It is an eternity, when you do not know
for one instant of time, whether the heart
that for twenty and more years has only
had one image there, and that one image
yours, is still; but it makes the youngest
in an instant old, when they must ask
themselves that word through nights and
days—is it life, or is it death? nothing
daring to think which. And there are
times when on the issue hangs, the drying
up, the withering, the living, or the dying
of the heart, that mocks itself to ask it.

Towards the evening of the third day
Reuben reached that, which, when he left

it

it was his home; he reeled up to the door,
and in the doorway Crispin stood to meet
him.

It perhaps was well for both, that Reuben did not ask what Crispin dared not
tell.   Reuben never took his eyes from off
his son, but kept them fixed on him, to
beg a hope, or kill suspicion.

"Take me to your mother;" and his
whole soul seemed to search his son as
Crispin tried to speak.

"Your mother, your mother, take me
to her ! Look you, Crispin, how little it
will want to make me mad;" and he seized
his boy's arm, and pointed up the stairs, as
though he did not know his own wife's
room.

Crispin saw that it would take very
little.

"Tell her I am come, Crispin. Tell her
—why don't you go—why——" But
Reuben Ken could see in his boy's face,
the truth which was written there.

He put his hand in Crispin's, and
                                        searched,

searched, as he had never searched before, his firstborn's eyes.

"I can bear it, Crispin—I think I can"—and he spoke this in a whisper; "take me there—*there* where they have put her." And Crispin passed on through the open door, till they were some way in the open sand, and there he stayed before a big rough stone.

"They are here," said Crispin, "I laid them here no longer than an hour ago."

Crispin from the first had feared, that what did come, would be; and it was not in him, to hope to keep his father's purpose back.

With his own hands, did Reuben Ken tear back the burning sand that kept him from the dead; it was all that was left him here, to see her again, before that she should change.

Crispin had had the coffin carried there when no one saw, and Reuben had come back to see that grave three feet in the sand. On the mother's breast, as in their sleep, the curate's last-born lay, and the smile that

that stood upon *her* lips in life, seemed chiselled there to him, as though it asked to rest for ever.

Crispin knew how it would be when his father stood beside that open grave ; and Reuben had the bodies of his wife and children taken to St. Hilda's.

Some very anxious friends, who were always busied about other men, were of opinion that it mattered nothing where the dead should lie, whilst it mattered everything that a curate of such little means, should leave them where they were. But tell that even to the man whose trade is discount, and whose eternity, if he could will it, would be the best of " paper." If ever he has buried what he loves, in his after hours, for awhile, *he* will even have a mind to stand beside the grave.

Reuben did it, and when in doing it he gave up his all, he felt the sea was not between him and the dust.

We do not know when life lies out before us, and we only search for life and living things, how often, long before the
end

end has come, we shall seek a churchyard at its close, or gather comfort from a
charnel.

Of course in **St.** Hilda's, where it was
easy for everybody to know what Reuben's
means could furnish, the more suggestive
and provident people had a great deal to
say.

The maiden lady, who kept house at
the Hall, was amazed—and it publicly appeared she was amazed—at the folly of
carrying three dead bodies at such a cost
about.

"What can it matter where we lie?"
she said; but, perhaps, it seemed to her,
that from her experiences in life, wherever
at the last she might be put, she would at
least be suffered to remain. Of course
the curate would finish as he had begun;
of course he would be setting up a stone.
Miss Strake would rather have no stone
on the top of her.

It was a bright evening, at the end
of autumn, about a month since their
return from Aden, that Crispin, who did
not

not know how bad things were, asked
Mona for some supper. Mona kept house
now, and was learning how to keep it
best on nothing.

"The last crust, Crispin, was gone this
afternoon; for I made father eat it when
he woke; it was very stale, and he could
hardly bite it."

"Never mind, darling, never mind; I
am not very hungry."

He was, when he said it, only just as
hungry as a man would be, who had eaten
nothing since the morning.

"I think that you had better fetch your
father, Mona," said her brother; "it may
harm him sitting on the grass in such a
dew;" and Mona went to seek her father,
where that father spent his days, and
where he would have spent his nights, if
he could so have willed it.

When Mona reached the churchyard,
Reuben Ken was sitting resting his head
upon his hand, beside the new grassed grave.
He did not hear her coming, and Mona
saw that he was speaking to the dead.

Reuben

Reuben Ken had passed in those few weeks to an old man. It seemed that he had aged a score of years. Sometimes, for hours together, his ebbing reason was as though, it would stay away for ever. Then he would get up, and, when no one spoke, would say that Edith was calling him; and he would go out for hours, and when his people met him, he would tell them that Edith was come back, and was walking by his side.

That evening, as all others, he had passed by the grave side.

When Mona touched his hand, and would have led him back, she was startled by the change that was upon him.

"I am hungry," he said, impatiently; "and don't you hear, your mother wants her supper; why don't you bring us food?"

Mona did not dare tell him why, and in a louder voice he asked again.

"There is none," said Mona; "there is no food at home."

At the sound of his child's voice, the dreams, he dreamed of that supper with
his

his wife, had left him, and all that had passed for a little time was real again.

"No food; and why should there be food for me? Why should I eat, if eating keeps me back from her? I will starve, and I will like to starve. Edith, I will come to you," and he knelt down, and grasped the sod, and buried his face in the clay above her.

And in that hour that man joyed that he should even starve. No food at home? Home! he looked upon that mound—he had no home!

When through a chain of years, we build up agony to come, and wrap ourselves in one idolatry, the love, that may be left in those who live, but keeps our torment fresh.

His child had told him that he could not eat; and Reuben Ken had come to this, that he was very glad. He could bear it; he could beg it, for what it would bring. He saw *her;* he saw his wife in that emptiness, and life in that void.

Mona

Mona would have led him home, but he did not know her then. She called to Crispin, and when her brother came, Reuben Ken no longer asked his wife, to come up from her grave to supper.

Mona had raised him in her arms, and heavily his heavy head fell back. Gently they got him home, and through the long night, in their hunger, watched him, as the fever scorched his skin. He had taken a chill in the damps of the dying day. The doctor when he saw him, could not say if Reuben Ken would live ; and for many weeks, the curate did not cease to ask his wife, to come up from her grave to supper.

CHAP.

CHAP. VII.

How the Perpetual Curate took a Chill.

REUBEN KEN lay a long while, asking his dead wife, to come up from her grave to supper.

It was soon seen that he had taken a chill on the high earth that was above her head; and that night, when he knew nothing, and was carried home, it was very clear, from many things he said and did, and from how he seemed, that he would soon be carried back to where he took that chill.

Weeks, and winter weeks, passed on, till there came that Christmas Eve when, as has been seen, after a long stupor he awoke, to ask for a bit of something he thought that he could eat—and the while
                                                there

there had very often been, as there very often had before—little enough in the curate's house for any there to eat at all.

A good deal of medicine, which it was thought would stimulate a little artificial life, had been got through the curate's lips. And it had sometimes done its work, and had brought back to him, as the past came up again, the power to think of the life that was still ; but the doctor, in his most sanguine humour, could only feel the tiring pulse, and say that Reuben Ken must live a little better ; and he talked of wine and other things to give the patient livelier blood.

He must have something that he, on waking up, could fancy: and the doctor, who knew nothing of the empty cupboards, did not of any sarcasm say this ; but the sons and daughters of the curate, who saw the empty cupboards only, were afraid that what might so be fancied, did not quite belong to sixty pounds a year.

The doctor, who saw how all would end, was at some pains to hint very delicately,

cately, or as delicately as such things can
be put, that the curate had, perhaps, better
make his will.

He did not see, that the making of wills,
had anything to do with living or dying ; he
held that men should think of that, before
it came that they had need to call a doctor
in ; but it would have been hard enough
for him, who held that cure, to have
made a will, whilst every day the little that
he had was getting less. He must have
conceived that he had, what he had not, to
have left it away. It must have been a
fiction, written in the ink of false pretence,
and he was much too near to death to
have the humour for it. A starving man
busied on his will, with nothing, always
nothing ! In his grave clothes he could do
that just as well. The doctor was not an
eager man ; but some one had told him,
that Reuben Ken held him in considerable
respect. The doctor was of opinion that,
if respect was to be evidenced after death,
there was only one material way of showing it ; and having himself a good deal to
find

find for a large family with great diges-
tions, he well thought this respect, which
he felt was very properly placed, should
have every opportunity of declaring itself.

He had brought all the curate's children
—except the twins—into the world, and
had had Jack's short leg to look to ever
since.

As he could see, without his good offices
being more than friendly, that the curate
had no testamentary deposition upon him,
he thought, as a matter of duty, he would
open the subject himself.

The doctor's faith, in what Reuben Ken
might have to leave, would not itself have
been very strong. He half suspected, that
what there was to leave, would be very
little amongst so many; but if the curate
respected him so much, there might be
something in it.

"I'm a little better to-day, I think,"
said the curate, as though he meant he
ought to feel he was, while yet there was
a void within that did not seem to bear it
out. "I don't know but that I'm a good
deal

deal stronger," he continued, watching to
see, if the hope he had no faith in, would
be cast back by the doctor's look—flushing
and then paling, and then sitting up to get
his breath, or some of it.

The doctor had known the man, whose
hand was in his own, for some two-and-
twenty years ; and he could not find the
word to tell him that if he was better to-
day, it was no sign to build on, or how
near he was to die. Nor did the doctor
want to find the word.

" There is more pulse to-day ;" and so
there was ; but it was the pulse of more
fever.

" More pulse," said the dying man, taking up the words, " more pulse—more
life—nearer to being back in the world
— nearer to that—but—further from —
from *her*."

" I'm an old friend," said the doctor, a
good deal moved, it should be said, against
his will, and feeling for his pocket-hand-
kerchief, " and one I'm glad to hear you
have some faith in. Of course, Mr. Ken,
it's

it's no business of mine, but the healthiest amongst us does not know when he may be summoned "—this was the safe platitude the good doctor loved best, and ventured oftenest. " It's not from any apprehension of an immediate change, but—but, it's no business of mine, as I said, though it's never well in this world to put off, till there's no holding a pen, arranging one's affairs. Your last will, Mr. Ken, will be considered in the disposal of your property. You are aware that in the event of—of your—dying intestate, your children will have every thing."

" And who should better have it ?" asked the curate, mildly, " they have been everything to me ; what I have, is all within these walls."

" Indeed ; I'm very glad I know it ; it's hardly safe—it isn't at all safe, Mr. Ken, to leave property about in that sort of way. God bless me—in these walls ! "

The doctor, who was nearer than he had thought, to what he fancied he might get, when he heard that it was within those walls, felt he would lay out a little more delicacy, in discovering what the property might be.

"If it lasts me out, my good friend," continued the curate, "why then I shan't live long, for it is going fast indeed; but, other than my children, I have no one in this world to leave it to. You don't happen to know any one that expects I should do otherwise?" asked the curate.

"Oh no; oh dear no; not at all," said the doctor, "that is—I only thought you might have some old friend, whom you would like to remember with ten pounds or so."

The curate looked very hard at the doctor to see what he could mean. To have remembered any one, who ever lived, with just one pound, would have asked for that, which he had not of his own to do it with.

"I've no friend in the world but my children," said the curate turning on his pillow, "only yourself and Mr. Wycherley. I have left you something, its—"

"Not

"Not another word, my good friend," said the doctor, "not another word."

"I've often wanted to speak about it," continued the curate, not heeding the rather demonstrative interruption—"its Jack's leg, I don't like to give it up."

The doctor of St. Hilda's, who knew as well as anybody, that there was no reckoning in this world on what any minute might bring forth, was, after all, only a man—a sensitive middle-aged member of the College of Surgeons,—and he would have been a great deal more than a man, if he could have sat there and heard unmoved, that his friend's legacy to him, after the delicate way in which the will had been brought up, was a lad's leg, that could not be got to reach the ground. He did not sit and hear it out unmoved; and he had almost said that he had had quite enough of so hard a limb; but the doctor was not a man who put himself at all to the front.

He had done a great deal for the curate for very little; having often come for nothing; but he was not of that sort which

calculates

calculates how many gifts they have given away; nor was he going to calculate them then; and he no longer remembered the will, as he took the burning hand of Reuben Ken in his own.

"You'll keep your eye on Jack then, won't you?" said the curate; "Edith had been very like to Jack in all but the blighted foot."

"Jack shall never want whilst I live," said the doctor, who spoke as though he forgot that he had ever thought to be a legatee.

"But I shan't put that care upon you yet," said the curate, wondering why he had come to speak so of those things, which might be only spoken at the last. "There's not so much that's ill with me now; but sit you down, I'm well enough to talk a little more to-day—you won't forget Jack's leg, eh?—but what's Jack's leg to you when I'm going to live?" and the curate put his hand to his head as the hot blood mounted there.

The doctor wanted to stay, for he hardly

hardly liked his patient's look, so he promised the curate that he would.

"Why don't you sit down?" asked Reuben.

The doctor thought he might as well, and looked round the room, but all the chairs were gone; there never had been many, but now there was not one. He could stand as well as sit; but when he looked back to the bed, he saw the curate's eyes were fixed on him, though it was not such a look as he could like to see.

"I told you that I need not make a will, that I hadn't much to leave, and that that little would not stay here long," said Reuben; but suddenly being minded that the doctor should not know how bad things were, he did not let it seem how great a strait they all were in.

And this struggle — hopeless, weary struggle—in the face of what we are, to seem what we are not, will never cease to mock us, and to canker, whilst, what we call society assumes to be so sensitive of being scandalised, by the coming of a

starved

starved educated man, to gnaw the little that is left him, in the midst of those full ones, whose greatest luxury perhaps would be to want.

And no one, even in St. Hilda's, where appearances had not the value that we give them further south, or further north, knew how very poor their curate was.

It was known that he had no great abundance ; but Reuben Ken believed that it would do the church no good, and might do it harm, if it was known that whilst the doctor said his life depended on his living well, he yet had even come to want for bread.

And Mona too, had put away from them the startling seeming, that witnessed the level they had fallen to. You might have come into the hungry circle, nor known how far away the last meal was, how far the next would be.

So they sometimes very nearly starved ; and if there was not a crumb on that bright floor, it was not because there were so many mouths to share it, but because the

the world without—the world that would
have talked—that does not like to touch
the things that starve—must not know
that the appearances it exacted, were at
the price of the hollowness it ensured.

So did the doctor—whose eyes were
some way open now—take his way home
that afternoon, still not at all suspecting
that he had not sat, because there was no
chair, in what was called a sitting-room.

It was some short time before Reuben
Ken and his family left for Aden, that
he made his first call at the Hall, but had
not seen Mr. Lyle ; indeed they never met
till Reuben Ken returned.

The Hall, which had been many years
untenanted, with its long rent-roll, had
been put up to public auction ; and had
realised, what those who had no liking for
it, called a fancy price. Mr. Lyle having
bid against a room full of very interested
gentlemen —who had come very tolerable
distances, having very considerable com-
missions—with an indifference as to where
the competition led him, which those

who

who had been eager to get it, and had finished no where, gave out, they would have been sorry to have shown themselves.

Mr. Lyle, who it transpired had only made up his mind to buy the Hall that morning, walked into the room about noon of the day of the sale, when the biddings were at 30,000*l.*, and going up 500*l.* at each offer.

"Thirty-five thousand," said Mr. Lyle, very quietly indeed, not as though he was there to show what he could do, if he was put to the trial.

Competition could hardly recover itself after this irregularity. The others, who were well-meaning buyers, liked the intrusion as little as might be ; and, although the auctioneer said that he could only take biddings of 500*l.*, they gave up the competition with very little good grace at 50,000*l.*

" I don't like his look ; there's something queer about it," said one.

" I can't see what he looks like," said another ;

another; "*he isn't to be got to look up;* but he doesn't seem like anything I ever saw before."

The only one in the room, who appeared to like the turn that things had taken, was the auctioneer. But the highest offer was 50,000*l.*, and there it stood at Mr. Lyle's last bid.

"I'm very sorry," said the auctioneer, "but 50,000*l.* won't *quite* buy this property; the reserved price is 70,000*l.*"

"I have wasted a great deal of time," said Mr. Lyle, who did not speak with any affectation, although the time that he had wasted was no more than twenty minutes; "I have gone through the form to give these gentlemen their opportunity. I have made up my mind to have the Hall, and I can go on if these gentlemen should wish it."

So had a good many more made up their minds to have the Hall.

"Seventy thousand is the lowest penny," said the auctioneer, addressing himself to Mr. Lyle, "and the deposit——"

"My

" My check is for 70,000*l.*," said Mr.
Lyle, walking away, as a sporting man re-
marked who rather believed he could supply
a telling commentary on anything in the
world in an instant, and had thought he
would buy the Hall right out because of
its trout preserves, whilst he had been one
of the first beaten—" I never saw a man
pay away thousands in that sort of way
before ; just as though he had as many
more to come after, and for a place that's
half to pieces, and which he hasn't fairly
seen ; and he did it as if he were paying
for a pennyworth of fish-hooks."

If that were so, Ruy Lyle bought everything that he did buy, as he would a pennyworth of hooks.

When Reuben Ken came home from
Aden, the first thing told him, when it was
believed he could begin to bear to be told
anything, was, that his old friend the squire
of the " 14 port " had been some time
dead. When the curate heard that Mr.
Lyle was still amongst them, Crispin and
Mona, for their father, went up to the Hall.

It

It was little likely that they would ever forget it. Mr. Lyle had received them as he received everybody. He was sorry they had not met before. He never saw any difference between father, and son ; between not very significant people, and very remarkable deputations. What he said, almost went to show, that he had had an interest in them and theirs very long before they knew it, and that he would never cease to have it. He spoke of Mr. Ken's long illness, as though he himself knew all the symptoms, and had been as very sick.

Miss Strake, who seemed to be dressed many years under the age she was, did everything that looked very cordial.

Miss Strake, if susceptible to definition, was what is called a "pleasant person ; " but in nothing was this spinster lady at all like to Mr. Lyle. Indeed, people said she was so little like, that the little likeness served a purpose; and this was why she was kept there, to show how many, and how clear, the points of the contrast were.

Miss Strake did everything very loudly.

She

She had a loud way of commending to the world the opinions of her " Mama." She talked loudly, and she laughed loudly, and said people were "such nice creatures," or "so ladylike," or, that what they wore was so "sweetly pretty."

When she was quite at her full, she would dart up and clap her hands, and those who saw it, said "she was so very natural." This mock enthusiasm really takes in better than half the human kind.

Mr. Lyle never seemed to want the right word, whatever he might have to say;—not that he of any necessity spoke to show how easily he came by the right words, and that he studied to get them—it was a power that was felt to be complete, but that was never felt to be acquired. Nor was his laughing ever over loud ; nor did his voice ever reach a tone within an octave of Miss Strake's alto ; nor did he ever say what he thought of those about him ; and you would have never heard him say whatever he might think. So, perhaps, as it was said, did Miss Aurelia Strake set her nephew off

to

to some advantage; and, whatever you might have heard of Mr. Lyle before you saw him, you were not in any way prepared for his presence, when you were before him in a room.

When Mona Ken first saw the white hair, and the white beard in the man of forty, and had heard him speak, and felt his hand, which took hers very cordially, the image followed her about for days. She thought that such as he was, could only live in books; but Mona somehow had no books in which they lived.

She had never known half an hour go like that; and she could only believe that half that time was gone, when Crispin motioned her that they must leave.

It was raining when they reached the door.

" Miss Ken, my carriage will take you home—or you will wait ? "

Crispin urged that the rain was nothing; but whilst Mr. Lyle was not seeming to detain them, the carriage stood before the door.

The absence of all show was quite the chiefest

chiefest part of Mr. Lyle's attraction. The man who drove, the man who let down the steps, must have been all ready to drive, and to let down the steps. Mr. Lyle did not give them cause to feel that he was doing them at all a service. Nor did he give them cause to feel, that he could get horses round from their stables like that, just for mere effect.

Mona said nothing for a little while, and when she spoke it was the rather to herself.

" I'm glad Mr. Lyle has got the Hall, he will be a very pleasant neighbour."

" He is very agreeable," said her brother, a good many degrees below his sister's enthusiasm.

" He is the most interesting person I ever saw in my life," was Mona's answer; " he is—what made you shudder, Crispin ? "

" Shudder, Mona, did I shudder ? It was nothing ; but you forget that you have lived here, where you have scarcely seen any one at all, the greater part of
your

your life, and interesting people do not often come to such a place as this."

" I can hardly believe he is only forty," said Mona, very little heeding her brother's answer.

" Nor can Miss Strake remember that she must be forty-five," said her brother, who had been talked to a good deal, on matters concerning the young, by Mr. Lyle's aunt.

" But don't you think him the pleasantest person you ever saw?" said Mona, who could only see the image, which filled her mind, standing there on the steps in the rain, and who marvelled that her brother's enthusiasm came so very short of her own.

" I would rather not say what I think of Mr. Lyle," said Crispin; " I do not wonder he is popular. I should have wondered had he not been so; but was there *nothing*, Mona, that you did *not* like about him?" asked Crispin, meaningly.

" I hardly know," said Mona; " he— *he never looked me in the face.*"

Mona

Mona had spoken what they both had felt.

"It *is* a perfect face," said Crispin, "perhaps too perfect; but I do not like to look at any face that does not, cannot look at me."

"Perhaps he didn't like to stare, and make us uncomfortable," said Mona, who felt her reason was not very sound.

"I don't think it was that; but you plead hard for him, Mona," said her brother; "and have said more for him in these five minutes than I ever heard you say for Wycherley."

"You would not compare John Wycherley with Mr. Lyle?" asked Mona, with surprise.

"That I would not. He is not like any one I ever saw. I have heard, and now I do not doubt it, that very few could ever be compared with Ruy Lyle. But I am not the less glad, Mona, for your sake, that there is so little room for the comparison."

The carriage stopped before the Parsonage.

age. It was the first time they had ever
ridden in any but a hired carriage in their
lives, and full of what their new neighbour
was, Mona sprang out to tell her father
what she could of Mr. Lyle.

What could be *told* of him was very
little.

"What's that, Jack? What's that
Jack's got there?" Mona said, pointing
to her crippled brother, who was strangely
playing with a child, which showed that its
too plain idiocy was very bad to look on;
and as it was trying with terrible eagerness
to assure Jack of its affection, the contor-
tions of the stricken child were horrible to
see.

"It's only Jim," answered Jack, carrying on the facial game, that seemed so to
the idiot's taste.

"And who's Jim?" said Mona; "take
care he don't hurt you," for the idiot
scowled at her as she spoke.

"It's all right," said Jack, "he's only a
little queer," whilst the idiot shrieked its
hideous laugh at the way Jack danced to
please

please him. "It's all right; it's Mad Meg's boy."

Jack Ken had too much to do at that moment with making himself into a toy, to tell as clearly as he might; so perhaps it may be better told, as far as it was known, who Mad Meg was.

Very little indeed was known. Everyone was always guessing, but no one ever knew.

She had come there when Mr. Lyle had first settled at the Hall, but, other than this, no one could tell who she was, or where she came from; and it was not much that Meg herself, in whatever mood you might meet her, would say to let light in.

But there are some people who will find out any thing; who will stay out of their beds to do it; and these people are not foreign even to the Cumberland border.

It was chiefly these people, who first set about calling the unaccountable woman mad, because she was so sane as not to care to account of herself to them.

The servants up at the Hall called her simply

simply Meg, and inquiry was somewhat
satisfied with the offered explanation that
Mad Meg was an old servant of Mr. Lyle's,
without all her senses, whom he permitted
to follow him about, and live off some of
what was carried from his table.

Meg herself said nothing to this, either
to confirm or to deny it; and it was soon
seen that she said very little to any one,
other than to Jack Ken.

The cause of this was not, perhaps, so
very strange.

Meg had always with her the idiot boy;
and Jack, who was very sensitive, and felt
that his foot put him out of the world's
companionship, saw in Mad Meg's boy,
something more likely to suffer such re-
proaches even than himself.

So Jack took the idiot under his own
care; and out of this had ripened the
strange liking that sprang up between
Mad Meg herself and Jack; and it soon
came to be that the curate's younger son
was never very long away from Mad Meg.

There was something in Meg herself —
something

something in the roughness that she seemed to force upon herself — that took Jack's fancy. He soon found out that Meg at bottom was the real thing.

Whether this woman, who was believed to be so wild, ever gave him any of her confidence, or told him what her past had been, it was soon pretty well the business of the place to know. Those who otherwise would not have gone near her, to have found out this, would have set about to try to tame her.

She had soon come to the curate's whenever she was so minded; and with some purpose, as has been seen, for Meg knew more of the philosophy of pawnbroking, than any other whose interest the curate could secure.

Meg was of as few words as most, and of fewer than most women in these parts.

It always seemed that she had something to tell, which must not be told, and that she might say more than she cared to say, if she said anything. But let Ruy Lyle be spoken of, and her tongue would
something

something run, if it happened that she was with those she felt would not betray her.

There was nothing ill to Meg's mind that Ruy Lyle was not; and Reuben Ken, who always made it a great matter to say nothing against anyone, even against those he most suspected, would gravely tell her of her want of charity.

Meg never answered him but once, and then she thought that she had set him down.

"Charity! is it charity you call it in the church, to see so big a rogue, and say you'd be sorry to think he wasn't well enough?"

Mr. Lyle had called himself, and had sat awhile on some three occasions since first the curate took that chill; but so well did Mona manage, that Mr. Lyle did not see how much they wanted, and how little likely things were with them to turn out any better.

It was after a critical relapse, when the curate awoke to the reality of knowing

how

how few things there were left him, on that Christmas Eve.

When the doctor heard how his patient was not to be over persuaded, but was so minded to come out of his bed and preach that misty Christmas Day, he said there would soon be an end now, to the long time in which the curate had been dying; and two hours after midnight, and after Crispin and his sister had returned from Mr. Lyle's, Meg went up to fetch him.

The curate had been put to bed, and the old thought had come back to him that he must have his wife to supper.

As the night went on the fever rose; and the curate, as he wandered and called on many who were gone, asked for Mr. Lyle. Mona, who was watching by him, started to her feet, as though to serve her father she would even then alone, have gone herself for Mr. Lyle. But whilst she thought, she felt Meg's fingers lightly touch her arm.

John Wycherley had never left that night, for the doctor had said unless the fever

fever could be soon got under, Reuben Ken would never live till it was day.

There was just a little dawn when the curate first began to mend; but he did not clearly know who stood about him. He called Mona to him, and drawing her to his side, said, so that all might hear, "I have dreamed that Ruy Lyle asked you to marry him. I do not think that it will always be a dream; but now you know that you must,"— and the curate fell into the only sleep the doctor said could save him.

When Mona turned round she saw Wycherley standing by her, as though he would have asked her, what it all should mean. "You won't think ill of *him*," said Mona, who left her hand in Wycherley's as she pointed to her father; "and could you hear that, and a great deal more, and have so much as any doubt of me? I have something to say, but I cannot say it now;" and whilst Wycherley felt it would be very hard indeed, to have one thought, that was not well of Mona, he a
good

good deal wondered, what she had to tell him.

After breakfast, whilst the curate's sleeping still let his children hope he would yet stay amongst them, Mona came to Wycherley, and beckoning him to follow, led him to the garden.

Mona had long been the curate's maid of all work; and what was all work there, would have given cause to every hireling to leave. The kitchen, as they passed through it, looked clean enough, and with Jack's help, under Mona's direction, every thing had a bright seeming about it.

"And now sit down opposite me, John," she said; for the day, for Christmas time, was warm; but there was not so much about for anyone to sit on; there were no garden chairs out of the sixty pounds a year; so Wycherley was forced to stand whilst Mona told him all, as well as she could, that had happened at the Hall the night before.

Wycherley heard it, so far as he feared what might come of it, to do him any hurt,

hurt, unmoved. He thought better of Mona Ken, than he thought of any woman in the whole world besides. It was a great deal to look into Mona's guileless face, and feel that whatever Ruy Lyle, or any other man might say, the heart whose first awakening had been his, had cast back the rich man, whose following, it had been said, was whatever of the world he cared to ask, to follow him. And Wycherley was now more sure than ever she was his.

But the perpetual curate of St. Hilda's the less, was a man whose selfishness was perhaps the least part of his humanity. He shared—and he did not conceal from himself that he did share—with the county, and indeed a world beyond it, an unmixed belief in Ruy Lyle. He did not indeed understand, what was the commanding influence of that man, but he did not seek to overcome it. It might have been sometimes that he wondered, whether if he were inclined to overcome it, that he could.

There

There was money that was not to be told ; there was a character that was not to be questioned—even within a circle to which cavilling did not come amiss—within the reach of the daughter of a clergyman whose preferment, at the best of times, left to him only a very decent controversy with starvation.

And what was John Wycherley, that he should perpetuate the respectable want, that had followed the father of that girl for two and twenty years ? And that father he did not lightly regard ; and it might be, he thought, that he could of some sort show this to that father's child, by doing better than taking her himself.

Mr. Lyle was in every way very far above what he could ever be. Mr. Lyle was a good man. Everybody said he was a good man. The world was his, and yet he was not at all the world's ; and this man had been no few hours before at her feet.

" No, Mona, it is enough for me ; it would be enough for any one of prouder stuff than I, to feel that he has failed where

I

I have best succeeded. He can make you, and will make you, Mona, what I cannot. Ruy Lyle is a man, whom the county has honoured almost before all ; and I do not think that any of that honour has been given wrongly. He is a man, whose principles have suffered nothing by those very circumstances, which would have been fatal to all principle in many men. Ruy Lyle does not throw his alms about the streets where every one can see ; but beyond such tricks to give relief and take some praise, he is the county's bene- factor, only needing, perhaps, the greater opportunity more widely to benefit his kind. He is a man whom to know is to reverence. He draws all sorts towards him ; none can hold back long ; but why do you shudder, Mona ? They do not seem to care that they are held there. It is exceptional, that an influence so great, so little hazarded,.and yet so all controlling, should be so wisely used. I sometimes think him, Mona, all that man can be ; but I sometimes wish that—it may be

I

I have no right to wish it—*he would look me in the face.* It means nothing, I know ; it is his way," continued Wycherley, perhaps not with perfect truth to his own conscience ; but it was the chiefest part of the indescribable power, with which Ruy Lyle drew society towards himself, that a belief in his unmixed influence for good, went beyond all others. You might have wanted him to look you in the face, but you were at some pains to assure yourself, that he had quite the best reasons for never looking up at all. "Mona," said Wycherley, taking her hand in his, "I think now, and I know I shall always think, that I should cease to care to live, if anything could stand between us, and yet—and yet."

"And yet what, John ? It must be something sent of God that shall ever part us here. This man draws me to him ; I know that ; I cannot help. it. You know what I mean ; it is something very strange, but it is against my will. I do not think had

had I not loved you, I could have loved
Mr. Lyle."

Mona could see that, although Wycherley stood still before her, within he yet
hugged himself with the thought of what
was his ; that she would be his, though even
Ruy Lyle should want to come between
them.

"Mona, I have some time seen, and I
have seen it more of late, that your father
does not look on me as he once did ; yes,
darling, he does not hate me ; I do not
think he will ; I know he likes me, and I
think he will ; but he likes another better.
He has looked the hope that was in him
before now, Mona, and last night I heard—
you heard him speak it. I do not think
he's wrong at all. If I must put the
question to myself, I must think him
right ; but your father would see you the
wife of Ruy Lyle ; and, Mona, you will
better judge my heart, when I say too, that
so would I."

Mona shook her head, "and could you

K 3

be

be its queen?" had had but an empty sound for her.

"No, no, John; you cannot give me back my heart. I have seen the Hall, and I have seen its master, but I could not hold that Hall with him. I have known what this is—and she looked round on nothing—and I can ask to share its emptiness with you."

"I had not a little hope, darling, that you would have so answered me. I do not say again, 'I, Mona, give you up.' I do not think I could; but I tell you, you are free. Mr. Lyle will be all that I could be, and he will be more; he will raise you to where you should be, and where I could not hope to place you. From this day, Mona, do not think that you are bound to me. I could hold you back to emptiness from any man but him. Weigh between us both. The world will say that an instant would be over long, if you are wise, to judge in. It is very simple. He has everything, and I have nothing. I shall seek out Mr. Lyle; something tells me that I must;

must; I may do myself some harm. I
shall bring him here. In a few days your
father will be asking, as his strength gets
less, for bread. If I bring that man here,
who may even take away the most from
me, your father shall not ask for bread
again. He shall yet want nothing, the
little time that may be left him. My
purpose is taken—answer Mr. Lyle as
though you never knew me, Mona."

"Will you take that answer to him,
John ? it shall be in words that nothing—"
and Mona for her tears could say no
more. As empty nothings were to her
the words of this man, Ruy Lyle; words,
that almost all the womankind of any
county, would have left their life on. The
choice that Wycherley would give her,
was to Mona Ken the greatest grief that
she had ever had to bear ; and had Wycherley, of his own purpose, so disguised it, the
image of Ruy Lyle could not well have
got more hateful.

John Wycherley could yet look proud,
and hold but one belief. He did not,

for

for he could not, think that Mona Ken
would ever take the freedom he had
offered her. But, he had seen too much
of what was very hard to bear beneath
that roof, not to leave her to her choice.

He did, as he said he would. He sought
out Mr. Lyle, and, within the hour that
he had so spoken to the owner of the
Hall, Mr. Lyle stood at Reuben Ken's
bedside.

"I thank you for this warning," Mr.
Lyle had said to Wycherley, as he took
in his, the hand of the man which Mona
Ken had taken; and, for the first time
John Wycherley felt, that he would a great
deal rather Ruy Lyle had left his hand
alone. He did not know why he should
shudder, but he did.

Mr. Lyle fell in with the resources of
the curate's wasting home, with a seeming
delicacy, that was not without its effect
on all.

None of the contrasts of abundance,
were suffered to mock the thinness of
respectable decay.

He

He came in such a way, that no one thought it strange that he had come. He said he was there to nurse the curate; and Reuben Ken, as he turned in his bed to say what his heart would have said, was at some pains to realise the better things that were upon him.

"It's a bad business, and he musn't stop, Jack," said Meg, when she got to hear of it. "If he does, I shall be in and out here oftener a good bit than he'll fancy; but never take your eyes from off him, and don't let John Wycherley leave the house."

And Jack did watch, as though his life depended on his watching; and he made it very hot for Mr. Lyle.

It was not found possible for Wycherley, any how to stop in the house. There were no beds, and if there had been, there was no room for any other bed to stand. So it was settled that he should come the first thing the next morning, unless graver symptoms should supervene with Mr. Ken, when Jack was to go and fetch

K 5

him

him.   Jack did not like the compromise,
when he remembered what Mad Meg
had said, but there seemed to be no help
for it.

There was an early supper, so that the
sick man might get a long night's rest.

Mr. Lyle was perhaps more cordial than
ever; and threw out all his influence to
please; and yet there was, however you
might criticise it, no seeming effort in the
throwing out.   It was felt to be a great
thing, for such a man to have left his own
great house, to take up his place by a
dying man's bedside,—a dying man who
was going very soon to die, and leave
nothing; but no one felt that he was
chiefly caring to please at all.

He insisted—and Ruy Lyle could do so
without much show of asking—on their
all drinking some wine, that he prepared
with spice, himself.

" Perhaps it is not sweet enough," he
said to Wycherley, who when he had
drained his glass, could not be got to
touch another.

                                    But

But Wycherley, who had nothing to prefer against its sweetness, soon after left, feeling a little headache, which he said, as Mr. Lyle was hoping he would sleep it off, was the penalty he always paid when he drunk mulled wine; and the whole house retired for the night.

The curate of St. Hilda's the less was not at breakfast; and when ten o'clock had passed, mid-day had come, and there were still no tidings of John Wycherley, it wanted very little of Mona's coaxing — she had herself been watching very long —to get Jack to go and seek him.

Jack found the curate in bed, complaining of hot pains in his head, and in his eyeballs, and of a still hotter tongue.

"It's nothing, Jack, tell Mona; but I'm glad she sent, and I shall be the better for it. I'm not so used to wine, and it has not done me any good—that's all—though perhaps, I never was 'like this before."

Coming home Jack met Meg, to whom

was

was confided some of the worst symptoms of John Wycherley's attack.

"What's the matter, Meg?" said the boy.

"What should be the matter?" said Meg. "I didn't say anything, did I?—nothing's the matter."

"Then you look very wild over it," said the boy, "for there to be nothing the matter. You didn't say anything—at least aloud."

"Tell me, Jack," said Meg, not heeding him, "what did John Wycherley drink last night?"

Jack told her.

"Did he seem to like it?" searched out Meg, as though a good deal hung upon the answer.

"Well, not so much as some of us, and Mr. Lyle did ask him, if it wasn't sweet enough."

"Mr. Lyle asked that, did he? You are sure? It won't do not to be sure of this."

Jack answered he was very sure.

"And

" And who made the hot wine stuff? "
asked Meg.

" Mr. Lyle," said the boy, " and he
made it for us all, and what I had, wasn't
so bad ; but what's the matter ? "

Meg's answer, as she seemed to be putting this and that together, was spoken
almost to herself; but Jack heard enough
to know that, what she said was, that
John Wycherley was very likely sick from
poison.

" Poison ! "

" Poison ! but I didn't say that word,
eh, Jack, did I ? "

" But you did."

" There mayn't be much in it, Jack ;
you musn't say what you have heard. He
didn't like the wine stuff, you're sure he
didn't like it ? "

But before Jack could answer, Meg was
gone.

CHAP.

CHAP. VIII.

How Reuben Ken made his last will.

RUY LYLE, had never again asked Mona Ken, if she cared to be his queen. It was not at all that he thought himself well out of any answer, but that Mona so contrived it, that she never let him have the opportunity, which it was quite the business of his life to seek.

Mona, however she might put it, could not say to herself that she loved him ; nor could she say to herself that she could have even loved him, had her love been free. But there was that about him, which drew her near—not, it might have been, in any way near enough to be asked so great a question, but just so near as to bring her very near his path.

She

She would have felt herself so much the
freer, had he ceased to live and hang about
her father's bed; but he hung about it to
her father's liking, and she could not
satisfy her own heart that any how she
wished him gone. And, perhaps, it was
not so much a question of the heart at all.

The strange, and inexpressible, and name-
less power, with which Ruy Lyle brought
all to like to feel themselves within that
power, whilst they dreaded that inscru-
table influence to which they committed
themselves, was rather a feeling of the
mind.

It was a great thing to say that you
knew *so much* of Mr. Lyle; but others
thought it a great deal better to say that
they knew so much the more. It satisfied
two feelings—that of knowing the most of
Mr. Lyle, and that of knowing more than
the nearest neighbour knew. When society can do this well, it feels that all its
education in that line has not been thrown
away.

Mona had never seen him other than
what

what the world knew him ; and, yet he did not seem strange to those impulses, with which he never appeared to be carried away. That magnified excitement over trifles, which to others seemed the highest order of amazement, only seemed to him to have reached that pitch when it becomes the most ordinary.

He did not reproach a jest, or seem ill at ease, because nothing ever moved him to anything beyond the merest smile. The whole strength of his remarkable will, was never shown in the evenness of his temper towards those with whom he differed.

It would have been felt to have been something of a relief, at which many would have grasped, had he ever betrayed that he was susceptible to the commoner passions. And yet, however he might bear himself, it was never said he bore himself with affectation, or that his earlier life had been given to the study of a part, by which he was to bewilder all he moved amongst at its meridian.

It was never said, however strange he seemed,

seemed, that Ruy Lyle was acting. If his whole bearing was irreproachable—whilst it drew every one near to him, and as near as he liked to have them—the power was such, which those so drawn towards him felt, was something which they could only rather understand to be against their will. And never had that power, so widely felt and so little paraded, been more strangely recognized than by Mona Ken.

Every morning, and every night she reproached herself, because she even took his hand. There was something in the touch in the morning, that bound her to return to its touch at night, and, that yet was as a chill, which stood on the flesh, and froze.

She even sometimes thought she did not like him, and that she would try to like him less; but she found it was the hardest thing that she had ever tried.

Ruy Lyle never seemed to be watching any one; but she felt that whilst his look was always down, he yet was always watching her; and if his eyes were ever raised, she

she knew that she it was who raised them.

She often came to think, as she hurried through the silent rooms, that she heard his voice, and heard him call her Mona; and what went against her to feel was that, had it been him, she must almost have stopped. She did not want to think she would have stopped; and she sometimes fancied to herself, that she was strong enough to wish, that he would have put her to the trial.

And Ruy Lyle, though he had never followed her, saw all he could have ever seen by following.

But from the power—she did not like to think it was a power—that was always hanging over her, she would hardly care to have been delivered. She felt that she could see the wretchedness that lay before her, if she did not shake the power—or whatever she might choose to call it—off. She struggled to hold back; but it was not a struggle that was very strong; and neither did she like the very emphatic interference of Crispin, and the woman Meg. She thought

thought she could keep him back herself, and thought at least that she would try.

Mona could not the while reproach her heart. The image of Ruy Lyle had not driven out the image of John Wycherley from there; but sometimes—and this some-times latterly rather grew—whilst her love was nothing changed, or nothing likely to be false, Wycherley did not gain by the presence of Lyle.

But Mr. Lyle had come from his own great Hall to watch her father; so when she asked herself if she should like or not like Mr. Lyle, she thought she *ought* to like him.

And her father, she could see, had some time given himself over to the influence that, those who felt it hardly talked of to themselves, and which was, as much too much, for those who were believed to be morally strong, as for the weak.

Mona, to put it to a test that finds but little favour with the world, not quite honestly excused herself by this. If her father was so very right, it was not neces-

sary

sary she should be so very rude. She
would not avoid Mr. Lyle quite so much.
did not want to like him ; but she did not
think she ought to hate him.

This was the power which Ruy Lyle had
never used grudgingly. He could quite
see how it worked, and how it would yet
work. He could see how she had struggled to avoid him, how the struggle ended ;
and he could see how she had hung back
by the way. He had seen the hand she
would have held away, and which had
every night and morning touched his own.
He could see that he was near to being better liked. He had worked out a good many
just such things ; and the curate too, long
since, was quite one with him in the
matter ; not that it mattered whether
Reuben Ken was for or against him ; he
could do without and against stronger
men than dying curates ; but, it so happened that Reuben Ken was very much
minded, that Mona should not hate this
Ruy Lyle.

Over this thing the curate was very
weak

weak indeed towards his latter end. The
one hope of his heart was yet to see Mona
marry Ruy Lyle. He did not stop to
think whether this was very fair, or fair
at all, to Wycherley. The influence of
Mr. Lyle, if it bore down those a great
way less susceptible, became an iron influence over the dying man, to which, as
his weakness grew, he the more listlessly
abandoned himself.

Mr. Lyle had now come to live at the
Parsonage. He never for a moment left
it. By day he was by the dying man,
whose weakness had now reached a great
way towards imbecility. Reuben looked
on Crispin, who resisted what he soon saw
would be irresistible, without caring
whether he gave offence, or where he gave
it, as one who would be always creating
antagonisms, for the great liking he had to
say hard things.

But, it was to Mona that the burning
hope within him was expressed; and latterly she had almost dreaded to come near
the bedside of her father.

As

As the strength of his body grew more faint, Reuben Ken would tell aloud his thoughts, even before Ruy Lyle and Mona.

He would lie for hours still, his eyes fixed the while on Ruy Lyle; and it seemed to Reuben Ken, that the man who came to nurse him did not need to eat, or drink, or sleep as others did. No matter what the hour of the night might be, when Reuben Ken awoke, Ruy Lyle was by his side, as though the earlier waking up had been arranged; and one morning the curate said to Mr. Lyle, "Indeed I cannot permit your health to suffer for mine; you must have your rest or you'll be ill, and then the world will be condemning me."

"You are very kind, Mr. Ken, but I have no need to rest more soundly than I do. I never slept better in my life."

The curate looked into the face, as he was sometimes obliged to look, although it told so little; and Reuben Ken was at his wit's end to know how such a man, could have come to such an age, if he had

never

never slept better in his life than when he slept so ill. He felt, perhaps the more, that it was a great thing for such a man, who did not even need to sleep, to care to be about him; and he purposed to have a word with Mona when an opportunity should offer; and the occasion offered very soon, for Mona, as she always did, came to ask him how he felt that morning.

"I am better, Mona; it would be a wonder if I wasn't; getting my strength, I do think," said the curate, wiping away the blood which had strayed to his lips, and told its story of the curate's strength.

"Ah! that's nothing," he continued, "only a little fulness of blood; I'm living too well; he makes me eat," as Mona looked upon that deadly sign, and for all that she could do showed she felt that it was deadly. "But what's the thing that does not please you, Mona? it is not such a lucky girl, I think, should look so sad."

Mona did not speak; she knew what her father meant, but she did not mean to show it.

"It

"It isn't because he is rich; it isn't
that," said her father, rising on his pillow
and speaking out the words his heart
would not hold there. "It is not because
he is so much better than most men,
though it might very well be because of
that; it is not because the country has
given him the highest place; it is not because—what is it because of, Mona? you
know what I mean—it is something, that
I cannot tell, which makes me want to see
you marry Ruy Lyle."

And the seeming ecstasy the thought
was to him, showed what the power was,
to which the dying man confessed.

"I loved John Wycherley before I
knew this Mr. Lyle, and I do not love
him less, now that I have seen Mr. Lyle."

"The love of Wycherley," said her
father, who would have defeated any object by the way he put his wish, "will not
serve you much; the doctor says he is but
sickly; if ever death was in man's face it is
in his."

Mr. Ken thought it would be better for
Mona

Mona to have been Mr. Lyle's widow, than John Wycherley's wife.

"Father, Mr. Lyle should not seek to make you speak like this. He follows me. He is always waiting for my answer,— that is, he seems to follow me. He—I can see his face now,—here,—there,— everywhere—that beautiful, that terrible face;" and she buried her head in the bed clothes, as though to hide out some frightful vision; and then she said—dreading to look up—"do not ask me to try to love him; never ask me to love *him* again, or you will make me hate him."

"Nonsense, Mona; you are learning to talk like your brother Crispin, who always fancies that he sees through everybody; and you shouldn't live in this world to see through anything. Wycherley is—"

"What Ruy Lyle can never be. Love *him!*—that face always searching and yet never looking,—that face—there it is— it is always following me; I cannot keep it now from what I dream," and Mona hid

her

her face, and Ruy Ryle stood there, softly asking something by the bed.

It was so whenever the curate ever brought the matter, as he had that morning, before Mona.

Sometimes the curate showed how little he was pleased at the way she spoke of Mr. Lyle, and said it perhaps was better she should love something that at any rate would live; but Mr. Lyle himself saw that, for the present, he would take nothing by moving in the matter.

And perhaps the strongest feeling now in Mona was, that she had come to see the end of the strange power, with which Ruy Lyle seemed to bind all he ever moved amongst.

It had been intolerable that she should be told of the dying of John Wycherley as a thing to be desired; and, as the sickness which had so strangely seized him, that night after supper, only left him now at intervals, to come back the worse, she knew that in his death the purpose of Mr. Lyle

Lyle would then take form, and her reserve to him was sometimes chilling.

He did not seek to alter it—not because
he had become indifferent, or because he
wanted time to alter anything; but, because his game had only just begun, and
this was only a chief part of the beginning
of the game.

His influence over her was not nearly yet
played out.

It was the one thing for which she was
always striving, that they should be never
left alone. She could not trust herself to
hear his words—words which to her were
so little like what they were to others.
She thought of the night of Christmas Day,
and knew what he would ask; and yet no
woman can feel that any man has words
alone for her, and in a tone which has no
likeness in its tone to others, and not feel
something moved to hear that which it is
her ever struggle not to hear.

Mona was one morning, against all contriving, left alone with Mr. Lyle.

He did not move—he did not seem as
though

though he meant to move. He did not speak. Mona felt she did not dare to stay; she had always thought what she should do if this should come, and yet, it somehow seemed to her, she could not go. Mona had always known that he was seeking this, and she had always felt that he would stop her—that he was always thinking how to stop her, and ask if she would be his queen; and what she had so long fancied would be, now seemed like a reality.

He *was* stopping her, or else why did she still stay there? Why did she not go? and yet he did not move or speak. She wanted to go, and yet she was still there. She stood up and moved a step towards the door.

" I know what you are going to say; but let me pass, don't call me back—you are calling me back now—why don't you let me go? '

"Miss Ken, there is some mistake. I did not call you back—I did not speak."

Ruy Lyle had never moved a step from where he was. He had not spoken, nor did it seem he meant to speak; but Mona had

had so believed he would, that she now
believed he had.

She saw what she had been led to do
the instant it was done ; but it was too
late now to say anything that could
undo it. He must have thought her very
strange and very rude; and she tried to
mend it by coming back, as though nothing had happened, and by sitting down
where she had sat before.

Ruy Lyle was not the man to show
what he might think of it, much more
that he thought it either strange or rude.
She felt very grateful to him that he took
no notice, or at least any notice that she
or any one could well have seen ; but he
could afford her this; he had heard all he
cared to hear, and he had seen all he
cared to see, as she came back and spoke
to him very civilly—much more civilly
than she had spoken of late—and said
some little, woman's, nothing about the
weather; and he answered her about the
weather, with not one word about that
other thing that she had said.

Mr.

Mr. Lyle never thought any occasion too small for him to excel; many men, however well they might have meant it, would have been clumsy over the confusion of a girl that had been so unwittingly betrayed; but he set her at her ease at once, and she began to try to recollect why she had once not nearly liked him.

After a little while, Mona found that she was talking to him on things beyond the weather, without seeming to think that it was very hard to do.

He certainly talked very well. She put it to herself that there was no real harm in being civil to a man who talked so very well. She had always thought this, so there was nothing very strange in believing it then. There was nothing new, she argued to herself, in the admission; and besides it would only be for once. She was quite sure what had happened that morning would never happen again; she would never let him sit with her alone, as he had done that day.

"I was going to see Mr. Wycherley, if it

it be fine," said Mona ; " do you think it will be fine, Mr. Lyle ? Meg says he is much worse — his illness seems most strange—it alters him so much. I never saw an illness alter any one like that before."

" I think it will be fair, Miss Ken, I was going to Mr. Wycherley's also," said Mr. Lyle ; " I have seen his symptoms before now, and they—"

" And they ?—"

" *They ended in death*, Miss Ken ; but it does not at all follow that Mr. Wycherley will die."

" Do you think that you could save him, Mr. Lyle ? "

" I do not prescribe, Miss Ken ; but if I were numbered amongst Mr. Wycherley's friends, I should be inclined to watch those carefully who nursed him. I could tell him this if you should think it well ; but you, perhaps, Miss Ken, yourself, will do that better."

He did not say that he should like to walk with her—that was not his way ;

L 4

but

but she could only feel that he meant it, and it seemed to her as if he asked it.

" I am going now," said Mona ; and whilst she would have gone alone, perhaps, had she been asked, she did not dare forbid his coming.

And so they walked to Wycherley's together.

Mona did not think that Ruy Lyle was very terrible indeed in what he said by the way ; nor after a little while did she dread, as she had sometimes dreaded, that he would put to her the question, she so feared, it was the business of his life to ask.

She said very little when their walk began,—and she walked as far from him as she well could ; but, after not so long a while, she let him walk a little nearer ; and she spoke of the woman Meg, and asked whether he thought she was a woman to be trusted with the care of Mr. Wycherley, a thing he did not answer very straightly ; and as they so walked and

met

met the neighbours, she was rather glad to be so seen with him.

It did not at all seem to her, that, as they went along, she was perhaps talking rather freely, and telling him such things that no lesser influence than his could have drawn from her.

After all, he said a very little, and nothing which it could be said had led her on; but it was just that little, and the manner of its being said, that set her at her ease. She had heard he could talk better than well, and better than most, even amongst great speakers; but she had never heard so many right words before. It was always the right word with Mr. Lyle; and yet it seemed to have found its place in the neatly-turned phrase, without being sought; and going down a hill where there were ugly looking rolling stones, and the way was slippery, and the walking hard, he offered her his arm, and Mona, quite because the road was hard, took his arm.

She had certainly, she now knew, kept

L 5

out

out of his way without any very sufficient cause. He had nothing to say that she did not care to hear; and how she could have ever hesitated to take his hand when he offered it so genially at night or morning, was more than she could tell. It must have been her fancy that that hand had ever chilled.

It was not two hours, since all the fancies of her mind had worked within her the belief, that she could not even pass her father's door because of him—that he stood in her path, putting the one question that she feared to hear, and held her back. He was not holding her back now as they went down the hill, at least in any way that went against her very badly; nor was she haunted with his face. It was not a face, at any rate that morning, fashioned to haunt at all.

He spoke to her of her father, as though the living or dying of that father would be a great matter to him, with just the reverence a child should like to hear. But it was not overdone. There was not too much

much liking; and he spoke of Wycherley
just as a man should speak who meant to
take Wycherley's place as soon as might
be, but did not mean to show it then;
and Mona was quite sure it would not be
a little thing to him if Wycherley should
die.

It would be hard to say how few words
Ruy Lyle laid out, to do the work he did
that morning.

"I'm afraid Mr. Wycherley is but
weakly, and that, though he gets a little
better now and then, he does not really
mend. Miss Ken, you must be very anxious."

Mona looked to see if his eyes said more
than his words, but they never did say
anything, and she remembered they were
never raised.

"We are all very anxious, Mr. Lyle—
his illness was so sudden, and so strange;
he is an old friend you know."

"It is well for him, Miss Ken, that he
should be reckoned so by you; but you

L 6

have

have not set him higher than his *mind* deserves."

Mona took this thing which was said by Mr. Lyle about the mind of Wycherley, just as it was meant she should. It was not hard to see that she was putting the mind of Ruy Lyle in the balance with the mind of John Wycherley; and Ruy Lyle very well saw all the balancing, and did not quarrel with the scales.

Mr. Lyle said nothing more that morning of John Wycherley, or of his mind, and he did not need.

They reached the curate's cottage about noon. Mr. Lyle remaining in a little parlour whilst Mona went to see for Meg and Wycherley.

Ever since Wycherley had been taken ill Meg had never been an hour's length from his bed-side. No one could tell why, though it was not many who cared to think about it. If a man, who lives on what a higher sort of butler would refuse to serve for, can get a hag to hold his head for nothing, it is not

not quite a popular concern how he may get it done.

As Mona passed on to where Wycherley was lying on a sofa near the window, Meg, in the rough way that had so long been tolerated by Mr. Ken and his family, stood before her in the little narrow passage.

"It's bad to love another whilst he lives, isn't it?" said the wild woman, grasping Mona's arm, and pointing to Wycherley's room.

"But I don't love him, Meg," said Mona, motioning to where Mr. Lyle was waiting; "and if I did," she added proudly, "it's nothing to you."

"Nothing to me, isn't it? may be it's more than you are like to know," said Meg, in a whisper, looking up and down the passage, "but not more than you may likely come to know. It *is* a hard thing to shake *him* off; but let alone what you owe to the man who is dying here, you may not—must not, Mona—marry Ruy Lyle."

Meg was always telling Mona this, and, however

however free the woman was allowed to be, this seemed going rather far.

"Marry *him*, Meg; there's no fear of that. I could not love him, were it ever so little, even if I did not love John Wycherley. It is not love that I could ever feel for him," and Mona shuddered, as she used before they walked together, as they had that morning.

"It's likely you won't always shudder when you think of loving him; and if you don't take care you won't be always thinking that John Wycherley's so much the likeliest. Doesn't that man there draw you on, you don't know how? Is he to you only what he was? Is he what he was this morning—two hours back? He will take your heart as easily as he took your arm coming down that hill, and then he will crush it, and he will still follow, for all he may crush. It's just as he will bid you, just as he bids all, and you won't have a mind to help it; and there is more work, mark me, here of his than you know of. Keep Ruy Lyle from here, and John Wycherley

cherley will live; that should not be so very hard a thing to do; but Wycherley, as he lies upon his bed, looks for this man's coming as you will soon. He calls him in his sleep, and it's you who have brought him now. Save John Wycherley, Mona, save him, and you can. You don't know what his life may be to me," and Meg laid her head on Mona's knees, and urged what she had spoken with her tears.

"I cannot stay his coming here. What am I that I should hinder *him*? Could *you* stand between the will of Mr. Lyle?" and they both looked round as Mona spoke, as though they thought to see the face they so little dared to see.

"But why musn't Mr. Lyle come here?"

"I should have to answer for it hardly if I told you, Mona. Let him come here, and Wycherley will die, and he will die soon. It may be as you will."

"If you want me to believe that Mr. Lyle would ever harm John Wycherley,

I

I cannot, Meg, and John Wycherley himself should speak, not I."

"He is bound—he is a fool—he is stricken, as are you, as once was I. This Ruy Lyle comes here, and Wycherley can no more stand between the cursed will, of the accursed man that chains him, than can the world. Lyle cheats by one long fraud. He, come what may, must not come here. You, Mona, led him here; you, Mona, you; and if you lead him here again, it's very soon you will be rid of Wycherley. I cannot tell you why, but see, there is not very much for death to finish now," and Meg, as she spoke with bated breath, led Mona up to Wycherley.

"You did not come alone," said Wycherley; "but keep away that light, for my eyes are badly burned already, and it seems to make the water hiss to drink it. But, Mona, I am better, and I always am when he comes here; better, to be only worse when he is gone. Oh! Mona," said John Wycherley, leaning on his arm, his eyeballs almost starting from his head, "what would

would I give to see *him* never here
again ; never, and he is so kind ; never,
and my tongue would cool ; never, and
this thirst might die ; but he comes, and
I don't know how it is, I'm glad he comes.
He gives me to drink, and sits with me
here, and something seems to hold him
here ; he is so little like any man I ever
saw before ; it's something I cannot fight
against ; something I hardly have the will
to keep away. Isn't he there in that room
now ? Ask him, Mona, not to stay—not
to stay—but I think that it may do me
good to see him for a little," and as it always came to be, Ruy Lyle was asked to
come to Wycherley's bed-side.

" What's that you let me always drink ?"
said Wycherley wildly.

" It's only what Meg gives you," said
Mr. Lyle, "it's her you have to thank, not
me."

" If it's the same Meg gives me, it does
not taste the same," said Wycherley ; " I
think that I could drink a little now."

Mr. Lyle smiled. " It's very kind of you
to

to think that I can make it pleasant," he said, taking up a cup by his side.

"Now, just taste this," said Wycherley, holding Mr. Lyle the cup.

"It's your fancy, my dear sir, that the rather flatters me I fear."

"But if it seems to do you good," said Mona, "you had better drink it;" and when it had almost reached the lips of Mr. Lyle she passed it on to Wycherley, who, as he always did when drink was given him by Mr. Lyle, drained it to the dregs.

"Don't go—don't go yet, you have only just now come," said the curate, as he rolled his burning eyes and tried to force a smile upon his scorching lips—"you must stay a little longer," and, as he laid his hand on Mr. Lyle as though to keep him there, and looked long and searchingly into the face that was as an image never leaving him at all, he whispered to Mona, as if Mr. Lyle should not hear what he said, "Take him away—I want to tell him, but I can't. What did I say?—don't believe her, Mr. Lyle—don't believe any one who tells you that

that I—I did not say to her that I do not want you here."

" I think, perhaps, that in his present state we are a little too much for him—we had better go, Miss Ken ;" and they went ; and as they passed out, Meg took her sleepless place beside John Wycherley.

Mr. Lyle, who had been watching for this, and was able to show he saw it, turned himself about, and Mona stopped at the sound of his words.

" I do not like the symptoms, Miss Ken, and less than any that rolling of the eyes ;" and, whilst he spoke he saw that Mona had been looking on whilst John Wycherley drained the cup held to his lips by Meg.

" As I said this morning, Miss Ken, you have cause to think well of his nurse ? I suppose that you can trust this woman who just now gave him that to drink ?"

There was not very much in what he said—suspicion admits of a great variety of subtle treatment, and in some circles has been brought to remarkable perfection ; but

but there was nothing much in this; he only put to her two ordinary questions.

Still, what he had said worked, and would work, and, from what Mona had seen, he knew that it would go on working.

Society has so well taught us how this may be done, that in its doing we may often even cheat society.

It was some few days later that the pawnbroker came to Reuben Ken.

Mona carried in the message, which was, that the pawnbroker had something to say.

Reuben Ken reviewed his life when he heard this message. He knew that of his concessions this had come.

The pawnbroker sat down by the bed-side of the dying man, and took the wasting hand held out to him in his. He began hurriedly, and in a broken way, or it may have been from how he felt, he could not well have got his words to serve him.

"You don't care for such as me now, Mr. Ken. I see you are well cared for; but I don't suppose it's the church you've got to thank for having better than one chair;"

chair;" for he could see that things of comfort had come up in the room; things which had not been seen for years.

"I havn't come for what I gave you on the coat. I havn't come for that; but I *am* still something hereabouts, if I ain't exactly all I was. It isn't the church that has brought me round. I havn't given up chapel, and it isn't very likely I shall, for that's what makes the most of such as me. In the church we ain't anything; we may have plenty to say, but you won't hear us. But in the chapel, if we know ever so little, that don't hinder us from talking; we are something and plenty come to hear us. Still I aint what I was, when I used to be against you over the way, and you wasn't much use against me. My voice isn't half a voice now sometimes, and I ain't got any breath like to fill a biggish room; but they tell me you are going, Mr. Ken; and you do look bad, and as though you didn't mean to stop; but I don't want you to go before I have said what I've had a mind to say a good
bit

bit since. It's no account saying you've been what you haven't been, and I've come to say what you may like to hear or not, as pleases you best, that you've made a pretty mess of this place, Mr. Ken, better now than twenty years. It *is* better now than twenty years since I told them that Sunday morning that there was no help for it, that they must warm up the chapel. Don't you remember that first Sunday that ever you preached ? Well, it wasn't likely that we was going to like the organ being set going, and you dressing yourself up in that white gown of a thing, and talking to us about your *authority*, and how the bishop pulled you about with his hand ; it wasn't likely I—who was what they looked to—was going to stand that, but now's the time for a plain word, Mr. Ken ; you are slipping away, and you won't be here to be told it soon. I shouldn't have done what you did if I had been where you was. It didn't ought to have mattered to you what we thought about it. We didn't go to get pleased, and it

it wasn't likely you could please us; and
we didn't like it a bit the more because
you began to put down all you had preached
up; and what a mess you did get in. You
didn't please yourself; you didn't shut us
up; you didn't do what we wanted; but
you set to work to show you was afraid of
your own likings, to make what you call the
church as near us as could be; and you did
it; and no one, that I could ever hear of,
thought it was a bit worth while going away
from us to come to you. There wasn't
difference enough; and that's just how it
was. It isn't likely you would have got me,
but there's many that I took along with
me who would have come to you, but they
didn't think it was worth while, as you made
the church so like the chapel, and kept
shrinking away from what you should have
held to. It's your middling sort that we
dissenters like; you who never stick to anything, but only want to make your church
as like our chapel as you can, but are afraid
to say so. You were so uncommon like
what we were; that's where you made a
mess

mess of it. I couldn't bear to see you dying up there on Christmas day; and it was what you said, and how you said it, about meeting every one of us after a bit— every one, and not forgetting me—that worked me up to fetch back that coat, and I hope, now it's all up, that there's no harm between us, and that you won't mind meeting me by and by, where there's no coats wanted to be worn."

Reuben Ken heard the pawnbroker up to the last word, and long as the pawnbroker had spoken, without the wish that one of those words should ever have been left unsaid.

"It's very good of you to come so kindly, and to want to meet me by and by. If I was weak, I did it for peace; and I hope that Crispin won't be harsh. I must have a word or two with him about it; there's nothing like concession in the church."

"If that's your son that you mean, Mr. Ken, I hope he won't do as you did; always meaning well, and always getting in the wrong."

"I

"I have seen what concession could do," said Reuben Ken, his eyes filling as he spoke, as though he even gave the memory up to fight against the giving.

"I hope it won't be seen again here-abouts, for a good bit," said the pawnbroker. "I ain't of your mind, but I like to see one thing or another; it don't do for us, and I shouldn't think it would do any great deal for what you call the Church. I like something well enough to kick against; but I'm sorry if I've ever vexed you. Twenty-two years is a long time for such a piece of work as ours; but it's all right now; perhaps you won't mind thinking of what I've told you; it isn't any dissenter that likes you a bit the less for sticking to a thing. One of what's called an "Evangelical" makes twenty of us by what he does, in no time;" and the pawnbroker, as he spoke, squeezed the thin hand that was so heartily held out to him; and he was gone to the curate, in this world, for ever.

He had hardly left when Mr. Lyle returned, to watch by Reuben Ken's bed-side.

"What is to-day?" asked the curate, anxiously.

"It is Thursday, the 21st of January."

"If I live till to-morrow I shall have been here three-and-twenty years. It's a long time to do no good, but to do a great deal that is ill, as that man told me I had done. I don't know why, but something tells me I shall not live beyond to-morrow. God grant that, even if it is to-night, I may be ready, Mr. Lyle."

"There is nothing I can do for you, Mr. Ken, you have arranged everything and settled all?"

"That was never very hard for any time this twenty years, Mr. Lyle," said the curate, smiling. "We have lived upon your bounty this month past. I have settled all, for I have nothing."

"And you have no last wish — nothing beyond all the rest that you may desire, Mr. Ken?"

Reuben

Reuben Ken looked with a long, mean-ing look, into the face of Ruy Lyle.

"I have, Mr. Lyle; you always know everything I want to say; it has been long on my mind to tell it. This curacy is—"

"I understand you, Mr. Ken; set your mind entirely at rest, Crispin shall have it, you have my word."

The curate pressed the hand that he always seemed to want to press, and yet which always seemed to chill him.

"I wish it were mine, to have the thought of having lived the life you have, Mr. Lyle."

And Mr. Lyle did not change colour, even before this wish of the dying. He never did change colour; but a more keen observer than Mr. Ken was might have then judged something from the smile upon those lips.

"And you've no other wish, nothing beyond this, Mr. Ken? You do not lay upon us what is very hard."

The curate moved in his bed towards

the

the man, who, somehow, seemed to search
him through.

"You know everything, Mr. Lyle —
everything you want to know — can you,
then, see through me?"

"It was only what I thought might be,
Mr. Ken."

"If you had not known it without my
telling you, Mr. Lyle, I should not have
told you this; but come near," said the
curate, in a whisper, laying his hand on
Mr. Lyle, "nearer — nearer — there is, as
you say, something about Mona. I love
John Wycherley; but I do not wish that
she should marry him. She might well
marry better; can you, when I'm gone,
see this wish respected?"

"It is a matter in which I would rather
not move, but as you put it, Mr. Ken, I
cannot well refuse, if you will give me
the power to act," said Ruy Lyle, in a
tone admirably callous, and which it would
have been generally said, even by the best
judges, showed how indifferent he was to
get the power.

                                    "Give

" Give you the power, Mr. Lyle ; I give power to *you ?* I don't think you can need it."

" You must make your will, Mr. Ken, appoint me your daughter's guardian, myself, and — "

" And no one else," said Mr. Ken. " This is what I wished ; you quite saw what I wanted."

The curate had exactly supplied what Mr. Lyle had paused for.

" I had better not act alone."

" I would rather that you did," said Mr. Ken, who thought it would want all he could say to keep Mr. Lyle to his resolve.

And the last will of Reuben Ken was made that afternoon, signed, and put aside by Mr. Lyle.

It was two hours after midnight when Ruy Lyle, who had never closed his eyes, went softly and knocked at Crispin's door.

" There is a change, and it is one, I think, from which no one in this house should be away."

M 3

" You

"You know what it is; you have seen death before?" said Crispin, starting to his feet to follow.

"I have seen some die," said Mr. Lyle; and as the light of the little lamp fell on his face, Crispin thought he never saw a face so calm—that meant so much—that told so little.

They stood a little later round the bed —all listening to the tightening breath, watching the change that was growing into death.

"He wants to speak," said Mr. Lyle, and Crispin bent over the bed to catch the words.

There is nothing in this world we strive for as we do to catch those words; some for the love they witness, more for the gain they summon us to take.

"Is that you, Crispin?—bury me by your mother—and Mr. Lyle has given me his word to be your friend."

Crispin looked round, and there was that in his look, which cast back on "the friend," whatever words might have been given.

given. But Ruy Lyle, as he stood there, did not seem to see it.

"And I want you, Crispin, to do everything for peace—always be ready to concede — I hope I always was. It's nearly over with me now; I'm getting very tired; I shall be *there* to-night with your mother and my little ones."

And the dying man, as he looked where the moon was sailing high, gathered up the little strength he had to bless his son. And then he moved his lips, as though he asked for Mona, then for Jack; and the cripple on his crutch pressed on to take his share of the last words.

Reuben turned to Mona, and took her hand, or rather seemed as though he would have taken it, and then moved round to ask for Mr. Lyle, and with the little strength that stayed, tried to place her hand in his.

"*It may not be,*" and Meg stood there to keep the hand of Mona back; and the sign of death had settled in its never-to-be-simulated form, whilst the living who

M 4

stood

stood there, took thought of things which did not seem to have death in them.

What was coming in the future seemed to them to ask for an eternity to fulfil it ; and each had added something, to the hopes and fears of their own being, before it could be felt that death was in their midst.

Ruy Lyle turned round to lead Mona from the room.

"It is better she should come," he said to Crispin.

"It is best that you should leave her to her will," was Crispin's answer ; and so did Ruy Lyle, as he fell back ; but Mona turned to take his arm.

"I did not *ask* it, Mr. Ken," said Ruy Lyle, as he led Mona from the room.

"Not here, not now," said Crispin to himself as he looked upon the still warm clay ; "but to-morrow — "

"And to-morrow," said Meg, "you will wish it were to-day, when you shall know his power. See, how he did *not* ask, and how she followed him ; and so did I a while ago, and that's why I am mad."

CHAP.

CHAP. IX.

A Funeral.

HERE is perhaps nothing which, under modern treatment, may mean more or may mean less than a funeral. It has long been felt by those who have made it a matter of business, how much may be done, and how much may be realised, over putting a clay body in a clay hole.

One man comes to die and he is buried by the country; and it is held to be of such interest that the reporters of the evening papers, who have strong feelings and are moved by anthems, are even there.

Another man dies, and, after a good deal of inquiry, he is held to be a subject that must be buried by the workhouse; and he

is, it may be, drawn along by a horse for
the first time in his life.

There is the gorgeous funeral, where the
putting away of the clay must needs be
very grandly done.   There are no effects
which an intelligent undertaker, if you do
not cramp him, will not secure.   But the
deportment of the mourners, the complimentary groups about in black, is very
hard to determine.   Nor has it yet ever
quite been determined.

It does not do for the complimentary
follower to be over cast down, or the inhe-
ritor of the name, or money, of what you
are burying away, is quite likely to be apt
to feel, that you do not think sufficiently
of what is left.

And after the funeral is over, the refresh-
ment—which is the same thing as that for
a rout—whilst the servants are pulling up
the blinds, and making the place look as
little like it did when the dead was lying
there, what is the proper thing for the
complimentary mourner to do?

Of course with some it had been thought
most

most worth while to send an empty carriage after the corpse.

The reading of the will begins the business. Everything will have been tending up very decently to that—the amount and severity of the black about you, and how you looked when the head undertaker, touching you on the arm and helping you over the ropes, told you the time for having the last look into the grave had come, had all been governed by how you believed you stood in relation to the will.

Setting aside those few to whom the loss of the dead does not happen to be a question of money, the complimentary long faces whilst they lasted, were about as real as the empty carriages.

It is not a little remarkable that you may have a general rule for your outward seeming at all entertainments but a funeral. You are asked out of compliment; you stay away from business out of compliment; if you are very much thought of in the city, this is the hardest thing you are asked to do—you go out of compliment—

you

you are found in gloves and in crape ; and you see two of the more serious members of the undertaker's establishment, unspeakably afflicted, on either side of the door, to carry out their employer's contract—their employer undertook that he would find two men to look grief-struck. But there are as many good things, communicated in one journey of a mourning-coach, as you will see in a month in a " funny " paper. You will have cast off the grief, that you took from the opening sight of the mutes, and by the time you are sitting down to eat and to drink, you have quite determined that a funeral offers to your complimentary position, a very fair share of what may be enjoyed. You have only made a mistake or two in looking too heavy, when the incident just occurring should have had a contrary result.

Complimentary mourning in our earlier education might be made an extra. We should be brought to understand the delicate medium of behaviour at a funeral. We are invited by advertisement to learn

how

how to enter, and how to leave a room, on
every occasion but after holding a complimentary place at a funeral. The way to
bury the dead is, after all, becoming a
cheapened and improving science. Those
impressible contractors, who only employ
the hopeless-looking, have lately introduced
a boot into the funeral machine, where the
thing is done by contract, and the dead
and the living ride in one black coach.
This cheap indecency is better than the
long procession. Everything is to be
made much of which weakens the position of the complimentary mourner. The
hypocrisy, that we take a life to make our
own, is devoted, in complimentary mourning, to the memory of the dead. The
joke creeps up when we come to mourn.
By the vault and in the waltz we stand in
the same black trousers. We expect too
much. The city man believes his many
friends will be his many mourners, and
that those who followed him will follow his
six Flemish horses. It is not that society
is any more sincere over our cradle than

over

over our coffin; but it may happen to be better worth its while to be civil over the child than enduring over the corpse. What it gets by going is what society will ask, and when society shall cease to ask it, may be only at the funeral of the world.

When it was known that Reuben Ken was dead, not a very great deal of complimentary mourning was thought to be necessitated.

It was not difficult to know that he had died worth nothing. A man who has had something to lose, and who has lost it, and who with the breadth of his operations has made others to lose, gives employment to his successors, in the great capacity there is for saying what he was; but Reuben Ken left no such capacities behind at all. He might have died worth something. He might have been doing what Sir Reuben Israel would have advised him to do; but he had lived his life through nothing worth, and he had died worth nothing.

So there was little enough to apprehend from

from the empty carriages that would follow him.

Indeed, it was very clear to Crispin that there was something very far from complimentary mourning to apprehend. The perpetual curate was dead, and had not left so much behind him as would satisfy the undertaker's meanest contract. There was certainly the bed on which the body lay ; that could be sold from under it ; and then there was the parish to fall back on ; but Crispin felt that the Church of England would never get over a parish funeral.

When he entered the room the next morning, Meg had already laid the body out.

" I can't make much of it," she said ; " it's a poor, shrivelled thing. I don't think he had such a fair chance as he should."

" What do you mean ? " said Crispin, as he looked with an anxious face upon the hard lines of the corpse.

" Mean ! Just that he didn't have as
much

much, as he might have had to eat, before he took that fever; but you ain't going to let Ruy Lyle follow him? It isn't come to that?"

"I have not thought about it," said Crispin.

"It's time you should, then," said Meg, "for he means to go."

"I shall order that."

"No, you won't order that," answered the woman; "he'll do just what he likes, *without asking*."

"Mr. Lyle has no such influence with me. I dislike him, and he knows it."

"You may do all that, and it's likely you do; but you'll ask him to bury what's here," said Meg.

"How do you know that?"

"I didn't know anything about it, only he wants you to ask him. He knows you haven't a shilling to pay the undertaker for the job."

"Has he spoken to you then, Meg?"

"He hasn't said a word; but when he wants most he never does."

"He

"He will not be so mistaken as to try; the intercourse which my father permitted, ceased the moment that my father died."

"You don't know that man, or else you wouldn't say so. You will never, till his death, be rid of Ruy Lyle. He will bury that bit of clay any how. You will forbid it at first, but you will not forbid it afterwards. By and bye he will be here — here, in this room. You will have him not to stay. He will ask Mona to the Hall till the funeral is over, and after the funeral is over; and you will set yourself against it, and you will let her go."

Crispin Ken said nothing that any one could hear; but he seemed to be looking back on him, who it was said could secure the every wish of his will, without declaring what that will should be.

"You won't always hate him, or think you hate him. I—I have loved and hated; I have heard him speak as you have never heard him speak—I have felt his power, when, to go on feeling it, I could have asked God to let me never die. I have worshipped

shipped that man, Ruy Lyle,—I have made
an idol of his image, and he knew I made
it, and it was not terrible to him at all;
he only liked to see my agony, to look at
me when he broke that image up. He
liked to see it, only as he can. He liked to
see me trying, as I did, to get away—to get
away from what? Not from what he said
or did; he said nothing, he did nothing;
but he seemed to chain me there; and you
will be chained, if he should be minded.
He has never failed, and he won't pass you.
I was not always what I am ; they did not
always call me mad."

"Stay, Meg, isn't he coming? I thought
I heard his step."

They both listened ; there was not a
sound that either one could hear.

"You thought you heard his step ; and
so used I—ever I thought I did," said Meg.
"It need not really be for you to hear it—
he only makes you *feel* that he is coming."

Crispin smiled at the fancy that was put
with so much force, and went to the door
to show the woman that she was wrong.
There

There was no one there, but in a few minutes Ruy Lyle stood on the threshold.

"I thought I heard your step," said Crispin, determining at once to put down Meg's illusion, "it may have been five minutes since."

"Five minutes since I was nearly half a mile from here; it must have been some other step that you heard, Mr. Ken."

Some other step; there was no other step like that which Crispin Ken could at all remember to have ever heard; but whether Mr. Lyle was speaking what was truth or not, from that calm and unmoved face he could not tell.

It was impossible for Crispin Ken to feel, however much he might want to feel it, that there was any great intrusion, or any intrusion at all, in the coming of this man. Ruy Lyle stood there with his hand upon the door, but Crispin did not speak the word that should have got him out.

Meg, as she turned to go, cast back a look at Crispin Ken, which was meant to tell, and told. She had said all along that Ruy Lyle

Lyle would come, and would stay, and he had come, and he was staying.

" I can't help it if he does," said Crispin, unwittingly, aloud. It had escaped him, that the power he confessed to be over strong to bear, stood now before him.

" No one ever could, and no one ever will, so long as he has a mind that they shan't help it," muttered Meg to herself as she still stayed on.

Crispin Ken felt that by his own act, his own weakness was proclaimed, and as he desired that its signs should be seen by as few as might be, he motioned Meg to go.

As soon as the woman was gone, Crispin determined he would have it out with Mr. Lyle. If Mr. Lyle meant to stay he should stand, for he would not be asked to sit. But as the thought passed through Crispin, Mr. Lyle evidenced how much he could do without asking, and he sat himself down.

" I shall have to turn him out at the door ; it will have come to that," said Crispin to himself, pacing the room with a betrayed irritation that most morning visitors

visitors would have found it hard to understand. "He has come here to offer to
bury my father—if he offers anything of
the sort I shall be at some pains to insult
him ; the parish purse is better any how
than his."

Crispin, as this went through his mind,
still paced the room; and Mr. Lyle, who
might have found it hard to interpret aright
the meaning of such remarkable exercise,
sat on and said nothing.

"You will be good enough to wait till
you are asked," said Crispin, turning and
glaring upon Mr. Lyle, "I can perfectly
well bury my own father."

"There must be some mistake, Mr. Ken,
I did not speak. I made no such offer."

"You said you would take upon yourself
the expenses of the funeral."

"Pardon me, when did I say so, Mr.
Ken ?"

"When ? now—a minute ago—in this
room—from that chair."

"There is some misapprehension ; your
sister will bear me out in what I say."

"Why

"Why are you here, Mona?" asked Crispin, who had not seen his sister enter the room.

"Mr. Lyle did not speak," said Mona, avoiding to give her brother any answer more direct.

"And if he did not speak, what was it made me think he did?" asked Crispin.

If the brother and the sister had chanced to look at Ruy Lyle as he sat there, they might have seen a smile upon his face that would have told them something.

"It often seems to me as though he spoke when yet he never speaks a word," said Mona to her brother, almost in a whisper. I often hear his voice when he is miles away."

"Mr. Lyle," said Crispin with a sneer that was meant to be very clear, "you seem to be possessed of an influence which you will excuse my not understanding, and of saying a great deal when you do not speak, which I think you should explain."

"I have heard that said before," said Mr. Lyle.

"And

"And you rather seem to like the mystery," said Crispin, endeavouring in vain to hit where Ruy Lyle was vulnerable; and at the moment he thought of having himself heard the step of Ruy Lyle, when Mr. Lyle must have been a good half mile away.

"You deny this influence yourself, then, Mr. Lyle."

"Is there anything strange about me, Mr. Ken?"

"Why don't you look me in the face, Mr. Lyle, and say yes or no? There is that strange about you, Mr. Lyle, that you look no one in the face."

Crispin Ken had set out with the purpose upon him of insulting Mr. Lyle. He had insulted Mr. Lyle; he wanted him to go; and yet he now began to feel that he did not altogether wish him gone.

"I was just going to John Wycherley's," said Crispin, taking his hat.

Crispin Ken had got no answer from his visitor.

Mr.

Mr. Lyle took his hat and walked towards the door.

"A minute, if you please, Mr. Lyle," and Mr. Lyle sat himself down again, bidden to sit down by Crispin Ken.

Crispin, as Mr. Lyle came back, could only remember Meg's last words, that Mr. Lyle would come unasked, and that in the end Crispin would ask him to stay.

"There *is* something in this man's influence," said Crispin to himself, "and, after all, he was a friend who my father trusted. I do not like him. I do not mean to like him, and I will not take his money, but if he will lend a little, it wouldn't look well for the parish to do it," and the more he thought of it, the less Crispin liked the parish.

But Crispin's hesitation, to put himself further in the power that he could not reconcile himself to, was least of all unobserved by Mr. Lyle, who took the opportunity to explain, that he had come there to see, if he could offer his services in any way.

If any one else had come there to do that,

that, and had spoken as Mr. Lyle spoke then, Crispin would have done what he wanted to do, and would have opened his heart then and there ; but he felt, however near he might be drawn to Ruy Lyle, that the influence—if it could be so interpreted —was not a healthy one.

Crispin Ken felt forced to go on.

" My father's circumstances at his death, will not be unknown to you, Mr. Lyle."

" Indeed, Mr. Ken, your father never mentioned the matter, and—"

"You had too much good feeling to press him at all on the subject," said Crispin warmly, and extending his hand heartily to the visitor he so little understood.

It seemed to Crispin that the hand he took was clammy, and had a touch he could not well define, even to himself ; but he forgot that he had not let his visitor finish the interrupted sentence, or a great deal of the seeming good feeling might not have been proclaimed.

" He said nothing about his funeral ? " said Crispin, who wanted to be rid of the

responsibility

responsibility of asking a man, whose influence he was perpetually combating, to
bury his father.

"Mr. Ken expressed a wish that I should
relieve you from all the liabilities of his—"

"As you so far had my father's confidence, Mr. Lyle, it would be unbecoming
in me to conceal from you that he has not
left behind him provision even for his
funeral; but this evidence of your good
intentions towards himself, and towards
us, can be only accepted as a loan."

Crispin Ken could have concealed nothing, had he been so minded, for Mr.
Lyle knew everything that Crispin could
have told him.

Perhaps Mr. Lyle changed colour just a
little, when Crispin spoke of the service
being disinterested. It was not lost upon
Crispin, who set it down to Mr. Lyle's
feelings, as the face of the corpse was, at
his request, uncovered.

"So soon, so soon," he muttered to
himself, as he saw the change about the
lips.

That

That was all that was ever said on either side about the funeral; and as Mr. Lyle went out, Crispin Ken remembered that the man he had once thought should never stay, had stayed,— had been even asked to stay; and that this man, whose power was so hateful, whilst yet it seemed so necessary, would bury away the dead.

Crispin had almost called back Mr. Lyle. He was angry with himself to feel that this influence, which he had so struggled to set down as nothing, had a great hold on him. But after the funeral there would be an end to it all; that he knew; only he was not quite so sure about it as he might have been.

It was under these feelings that, as he was leaving the room, Mona touched him on the arm.

"Crispin, you know what *his* influence is now."

"I know nothing about it. I want to know nothing about it. I don't know, moreover, what you mean by this man's influence.

N 2

influence. Is he so unlike all other men ? "

Crispin had started a question which he had put to Ruy Lyle, and which he had hardly liked himself to answer. It said all that could be said of the man whose influence was just then paramount throughout the country.

" I think he is," said Mona. " He comes here, and I know that he is coming when he is not near. I am sure I will not see him, yet I see him. I know what he will say, and think how I will answer it, but somehow *so*, I do not answer it. I do not know what it is, Crispin ; it makes me very wretched, yet everybody says he is so very good. I only feel it is an influence I cannot and I do not like, but that I have no power to resist. There is some mystery about him. He never speaks of what he did when he was young. When he was here just now he *said* almost nothing ; but I know he did everything he wanted."

" His coming here amongst us, Mona, was mysterious. The way he bought the

Hall

Hall — the way in which he looks no one in the face. I never like such great, good men ; but my flesh creeps, — I cannot help its creeping when I think of him. After the funeral, Mona, we shall never see him again — at least — well — why do you look so, Mona ? "

" I think that that depends on what his will may be," said Mona, as she left the room.

Crispin stayed behind a little while to think, and the chiefest thing he thought was, that to be under such an influence as this, could be only what the weak would acknowledge to. It should not be thought that he was under it after the funeral.

It was after the funeral now. During the week that the body lay in the house, Mr. Lyle's attention to the curate's family had never seemed like an attention to them. It seemed, as though the favour done, was rather done to him. They wanted no-thing ; — it was all supplied before they wanted it ; — and Crispin found himself, he hardly knew why, taking from Mr. Lyle,

what

what he could ill deceive himself into fancying was a loan.

Crispin, and Jack, and Mr. Lyle, were the only mourners at the funeral. A great many people were sorry Mr. Ken was dead, for he had had a kindly way about him; but they had never known him as a churchman. He had been at life-long pains that they should not know him so; and as a belonging of the Church they were not going to follow him.

"I have a great deal to thank you for, Mr. Lyle," said Crispin, with the unsuspecting heartiness which belonged to his nature. It is always so. Those that are accredited with the least, of what the world calls "charity," do not see motives, when the "charitable" about them can only suspect.

Crispin Ken suspected Ruy Lyle of not being what he seemed. He suspected that advertised goodness, which was an influence and a belief received by all; but he did not think that that week's sympathy could have an end beyond; and Crispin would

would have said what it was quite in his heart to say. Mr. Lyle saw what was meant and stayed the words.

"We must part here, Mr. Lyle," said Crispin, as they stood before the parsonage.

Mr. Lyle, just then, did not care to probe the meaning of what Crispin said.

"We shall see you all at the Hall to-day, Mr. Ken?"

"Not to-day, if you please, Mr. Lyle," and not to-morrow, Crispin had it on his lips to say.

"It is most general that such things should be done at once; I think, indeed, on the day of the funeral," said Mr. Lyle, who never accepted a direct issue upon anything.

"I do not understand you, Mr. Lyle. You have buried my father, I can never forget your sympathy; but, other than this, there is nothing now between us."

"I think that we should see what are your father's wishes, Mr. Ken."

"I think that I should best know what

they

they are, Mr. Lyle. He did not ask your
sympathy to go beyond his funeral; after
that I only know his wishes."

"And yet he left their writing-out to
me."

"The writing-out of what, Mr. Lyle?"

"You do not seem to know, Mr. Ken,
that your father, the late curate of this
parish, made a will; and that, after the
funeral, is generally the time to let the
wishes of the dead appear."

Crispin had more than he very well could
bear, to think that Mr. Lyle should have
known anything about his father, that he,
that father's son, knew nothing of. That
was bad enough; but, that his father should
have made a will, and that it should be
only known till now to Mr. Lyle, was
nothing tolerable at all. It would have
been something easier to bear if Mr. Lyle
had seemed to triumph in the monopoly
of confidence. But he did not seem. It
was hard to fall foul there.

"And the will is with me," said Mr.
Lyle; "you might like to see it."

"It

"It is strange that I should not have heard of it."

Mr. Lyle did not at all seem to think it was. "You see, Mr. Ken, it was only made the afternoon your father died."

"It was by your influence," said Crispin, seeing, as he thought, his way to force a quarrel ; "besides, it is not witnessed."

"It was by your father's own request," said Mr. Lyle, who never had been seen to quarrel, "and it was witnessed, as you will have an early opportunity of seeing, by two of my own tenants who were passing by. It is very short, and appoints me executor, and guardian of your sister.—Miss Ken will have her own apartments at the Hall."

Crispin's fingers itched, but he did not believe he had heard rightly. Ruy Lyle the guardian of his sister ! But it was no use to be other than as cool as Mr. Lyle ; that man should not see how much he cared, or that he cared at all.

Without its seeming how it came about, Ruy Lyle was once more in the parsonage.

He

He was never to have stood there again after the funeral; and Crispin Ken had almost thought there must be something in the power of this man to make things worse.

Mona had entered the room, and had heard something about the making of her father's will.

" You perhaps, Miss Ken, at least, will spend this evening at the Hall. We shall be alone," said Mr. Lyle, who thought this was the best way of putting it till the will was proved.

" Mr. Lyle, you must see that we can only give one answer. You make us feel the obligations that we have been compelled to put ourselves under to yourself."

" Perhaps Miss Ken will like to see the home I have to offer her."

" I shall answer for my sister for the present, Mr. Lyle."

" I would rather stay with you," said Mona.

" You will have heard that, Mr. Lyle," said Crispin.

Mr. Lyle never stayed anywhere too long.

long. He had got his answer, and he moved towards the door.

"I do not think we ought to refuse," said Mona to her brother.

"Did you speak, Miss Ken," said Ruy Lyle, stopping, with his hand upon the door.

Mona said nothing, but Crispin felt that the mischief had been done.

"It is miserable weakness, Mona," said her brother; and she would have thought so all the more had she but seen how Ruy Lyle was watching her.

"Where should we have been without him this last week?" continued Mona. "It perhaps may seem we do not thank him;" and she said this so as it could be heard alone by Crispin.

"You want to go, Mona, whilst you only think you want to stay. It is a cursed power hanging over us that shall not last beyond this night," was her brother's whispered answer.

"Mr. Lyle, we thank you, and will pass this evening at the Hall."

N 6

The

The evening passed away, and Mona only went there, specially confided to Miss Strake.

"You saw but half when you were here before, Miss Ken," said Mr. Lyle, taking up his lamp some time after tea.

Mona had seen enough, and she wanted to say so; but she could not find the word. She followed, and before an hour was gone was in the long drawing-room, just where she had been upon the night of Christmas Day. She had never so felt the power of this man before. He had been just what it is well to be after a funeral. He had not said one thing that jarred with any thought of the dead, but yet he had said nothing that should let her despond; and the scene of Christmas Day, which had haunted her ever since, was before her again; and the sound of his words rung in her ears just as they had then. She could almost have kneeled before him, unimpressible as he was; and beyond the purpose that she feared she felt, she could have done anything if he would

not

not speak those words again; and yet
whilst there was no seeming that he
wanted to detain her, it would have been
a comfort to her to have been with Miss
Strake, and Mona felt as though she was
held there. Why had she come there?
Why had she followed him? She could
not give a reason, even to herself, for whatever she might do at this man's silent
bidding.

"Mr. Wycherley is better, and yet I
do not think that he can be better long.
It surprises me your father did not like
him," said Mr. Lyle.

"There was no man my father ever
better loved."

"And yet, Miss Ken, that liking is not
written here," and Mr. Lyle held out the
will, which Mona read in agony.

"He did not know what he was saying;
my father always loved John Wycherley."

"And if John Wycherley should die?"
And Ruy Lyle asked of her this question,
as he could ask a thing when he was
minded. "And if John Wycherley should
live,

live, you would not love, Miss Ken, the man your father could not like; *and if John Wycherley should die?*"

"John Wycherley may die to-night," said Meg, who stood before them, as she had on Christmas night.

"Is he very ill?" said Mona, with her hand upon the door.

"He cannot very well be worse," said Meg.

Mona heard no more; she bade her host good night, and begging him to do so for her to Miss Strake, though it was nearing midnight, she hurried down the road that led to Wycherley's, Meg finding it a little hard to keep as near her as she would.

He hardly knew her when she stood beside him, but afterwards he did; and it was with him, as it always was, he wanted terribly to keep away the very name of Ruy Lyle, but could not set aside the torment of that man's image which was ever there.

"I have heard it all," said Wycherley, "may

" may God give me strength to bear it;
your father, Mona, bids you hate me."

" No! no! he never did bid that; and
if he could—"

" And if he could ? "

" And if his curse had waited on the
answer, he could not have made me love
the less, or hate the more. And so I
would have told him, Ruy Lyle, just now,
when he asked me what I should say to
him if you should die."

Wycherley held his hot and heavy head,
and turned his burning eyes to look in
Mona's face, and death or life were staked
on what he read there.

" If I should die ? And is this then all
to end in death ? Keep him away, and I
shall live. Mona, you will say those words
again, that never whilst you live you will
ever marry Ruy Lyle."

Mona knelt down by his side to say it
after him.

" Never—never! but his face—it's here,
it's there, looking, Mona, on me now."

And Ruy Lyle himself stood there
before them.   CHAP.

CHAP. X.

The " Evangelicals."   A Saturday Review.

CRISPIN KEN had always hoped to be a clergyman.   He had been very well able to see, what sort of a fight his father had made of it those two-and-twenty years on sixty pounds a year; but he did not think he should be wanting in strength to do it himself.

Crispin Ken was not at all going to do as his father had done.   He meant to see whether his father was quite right—or right at all—in giving away so much to the dissenters.   It is the only tolerable thing, to talk of " conscientious objections;" but Crispin Ken had seen a very considerable something of the selfish cant which such could cover.

The

The cure in his father's keeping had been nearly lost.

Crispin Ken sought nothing — nothing but the opportunity of getting back a part of that to the Church, which Reuben Ken, in his amiable infirmity, had carried away.

Some people might call this "extreme;" but Crispin Ken would make over to such the gift of calling it whatever they pleased. It can only be seen in his after life what came of his purpose.

He had just then to present himself before his bishop; and after having got through the bishop's Calvinistic chaplain's apology for the Liturgy, say he believed this and subscribed to that.

It is a serious thing sometimes to believe anything. That experience must be at least a narrow one, which has not seen this even instanced in the child, as it comes up tired from its toy and shakes its little head, when all its mother's care was to get it to spell over little stories in one syllable that "God is good." Over the story book there was no dispute perhaps about

about it; but if God was good, the child
would think why had God taken his papa
away, when he had heard his mamma ask
God very often not to take him. And
this belief, in certain things necessary to
ordination, and the subscription to certain
other things equally demanded, does not
prevent a belief that you have subscribed to
something tolerably near the heretical, and
have announced a belief in something
wrong. The child may often say, when
unconvinced, it believes that God is good,
because it is not too old to like to see its
mother always smile; but it *does* not
nearly always quite believe. There is a
good deal of infidelity about in spencers
and pinafores.

The candidate for ordination gives out
that he believes the Thirty-nine Articles
ought to be thirty-nine, when he is just
going to print a pamphlet which is to show
that they ought to be only about thirty-
seven. And very little will come of it if
you take any action on his pamphlet. The
candidate has only become the curate; and
the

the bishop, who has laid his hands upon him, it is very likely, has no greater belief that the Articles are neither too many nor too few than has the curate.

They think nothing of baptismal regeneration, and spiritualise it to death on the first opportunity. They subscribe to it as a matter of some necessary form. The chaplain who examined them had evidently, in his mild way, strong " views" against it. The bishop had strong " views" against it —very strong if he be at all of late creation. There is no need to believe in it or in any part of it; and there is no need to say you do after a little while.

But you can never mend this in these days of " civil and religious liberty." Indeed, it seems very necessary to " evangelical" propagandists that you do not mind to mend it. You can make the subscription what you please, and then write as many essays or reviews against the Bible, as it is, as you may like ; but you cannot make him faithful who, as a bishop, believes apostolic succession, for his own purposes,

poses, a mere convenient sham, and Episcopacy a lie in lawn.

People in these compromising times know better than to interfere with unfaithful bishops. It would not do to seek to set down one's latitudinarian friends, or the world might get unsafely thin. It does not pay to keep men up to what they have professed. It would be looked upon as "Anglican intolerance;" and Exeter Hall would contract to send about some half dozen men, to stagger through the streets between two boards, to call "Protestantism" together in the lower room.

A man subscribing to baptismal regeneration and absolution, called to account for saying how little he believed in either! Such persecution would be overset at once. There are ever so many ways of oversetting it. The "Evangelical Alliance," whatever it may be, would probably meet and express opinions, and this would be considered to show that Protestant liberty at any rate was safe.

In the general offering, if this might have

have been freely interpreted, it would still be something as the record of the views of "evangelical" elders. Then those gentlemen of these evangelical "views," who may happen to have heard that a religious peer meant, if he was spared, to make them bishops, would be very active. An unfaithful "evangelical" bishop is not to be reached in any way yet known. He preaches against the belief of his own subscription. He denies the authority that made him a bishop; but he does not deny that he likes what he has got, and that he means (D.V.) to keep it. And what will you drive him from?—what he will confess to. What will you extort?—his own apology for his own office.

If you have a great deal of simplicity, and cathedrally attend the consecration of bishops, you will hear him say that he believed in this and subscribed to that. If you were rather young you thought he meant it. But this shows how great a wrong you did the "evangelical."

Any how the development of unadulterated

terated " evangelical " Protestantism is not
by any negative action. It may happen that
a man can do some unintended good in
the world to the cause he serves, by being
unfaithful ; but " evangelical " Protestantism, if it can help it—and under late ad-
ministrations it has been helped to do a
good deal in this way—won't let anybody
else be faithful.

And it is remarkable what it has done,
by talking on religious nights in charity
schools, when a text over the door has taken
the place of the price of admission, of the
danger of " extreme ritualism." If it happens to have arranged for the appearance
of any one easily inflamed, "extreme ritualism " will be made to mean, in the end,
many fanciful things. The subject will
be treated in allegory and in anecdote, and
the prayer-book, as it should be, sent round
the room.

Some tradesman or another, who wants
to push his business inexpensively, will be
made churchwarden, and a deputation to
the bishop will show the world outside
that

that but for them, the Church of England would be in a very poor way. This only shows how much this Church can stand. The churchwarden will not object to move a resolution for the " revision of the Liturgy," with all the epithets of Calvinism put into his mouth, if he can see his way to getting rid of the stock of unrevised books of Common Prayer he has on hand. Perhaps this is the best thing "Evangelicalism" could do. It might be inconvenient to prove that it is very faithful in anything, or faithful at all.

It is not a very remarkable body that reads the" Record;" but it would even cease to be conspicuous at all if it did not read the " Record."

" Evangelical " Christianity, in its integrity, if it means anything, means that the ritual is simply nothing. But " Evangelicalism " would have been very unlike what it is, if it could have satisfied itself by eating the bread of its applauded unfaithfulness in at all a decent way. Like an unclean eater over his meat, it must

make

make a noise, and show the food in mastication in its mouth.

Everybody, it is asserted, who may see anything in the ritual but a thing to be betrayed, is dragging the Church to the Vatican. The platform locomotion is inevitably " dragging." Then they made a religious peer, who was well connected, absolute ; and set to to pack the bench of bishops; and of this it was to come that the ritual was to be " revised."

But the great hit was to be over the baptism. They called themselves " Evangelicals," meaning to carry on their trade under an entirely unobjectionable name; and the thing has not been wholly unsuccessful. There well may be no need to show how much more the Church can bear—the minor theatres are the hope of schism, and an increase in the episcopate must give a see to Sadler's Wells.

Many bishops have lately died, and popular preachers, who learnt very little at school, and who have learnt less by their experience, have been distributed about at the instance

of

of one not very remarkable man, to " put down the ritual." You cannot very logically ask *them* to interfere with the man who has subscribed to the Thirty-nine Articles, and never ceases to set himself against just what it may please him of that number.

"Evangelical Protestantism" has made its bishops about the last hope of the Church, against those little caring to be faithful. It is a bad business to ask such as they are to interfere. What, for their comfort, can they do ? They will tell you that heaven is not to be reached by so many stops to an organ, or by so much music. They will almost tell you that there is not so much music as is supposed in heaven ; and because you may want to be let to do, what the least exaggerated reading of the ritual orders, they will tell you where " this extreme ritualism" will lead you.

This is what it has got to. " The faithful are perishing out of the land." It was David who said this ; and David sat all day before a harp, and hung a white thing about him ; people who sing so much must take

the consequence. The consequence they
must take is that what David " sung," is
" said." But if you seek out one of these
bishops to get him to interfere, and annoy
a churchman, he will see a great many
reasons for the interference. He will order
him to clear away the little boys in white,
and to " say " the psalms, and always to
deliver himself of his " discourse " in black,
and not to say too much about absolution,
and not to insist on baptismal regeneration.

It is quite an understood thing that you
will be told all this, and more like it if you
should go to any of those bishops, who are
considered sound, to set down a churchman.

If there be any one accidentally near,
likely to put it in the *Record*, he will tell
you that episcopacy is a belief that may be
overvalued. It will not be denied that a
man's success in orders now, almost ceases
to be a matter of speculation. To be
either " evangelical " or dull, is to be one
of these bishops' chaplains. To be both,
is to be one of these bishops. A new
bishop is always anticipated, unless a worse
man

man has been overlooked. "Evangelical"
Protestantism, so far, is not very exacting.
It asks for nothing in those it honours. It
has only lately occurred to the "Evangelicals" that while it is no matter that
they be faithful—though it is necessary to
their existence that they be *not* faithful—
they may as well cease to subscribe to what
they so very decently betray.

"Liturgical revision" can only make
these gentlemen easy. They can then put
all churchmen down ; and they have got it
recognised as an offence, inspired by that
remarkable platform terror, the Scarlet
Lady, for any clergyman to give effect to
the professions of his ordination.

It has been rather suspected that the
" Evangelicals," for those who take so
much, know very little ; but they have
some time known how to rise on the belief that they despised, and to keep there
by what they have betrayed. They have
been some time satisfied that it should
have been convenient ; but now they want
it to be made respectable.

o 2

This

This was the situation of which Crispin took the bearings in a Saturday review. It was the first Saturday since his father's funeral ; and the little that they had, was growing so small, he felt he must be doing something.

He had always meant to be a clergyman. He did not mean to show those who might look on, and risk hard comparisons, that his father had done a multitude of wrong things, quite meaning to do as many that were right. People would say that he had a mind to be " extreme." They were saying it already ; but he quite purposed, that those who wanted to see if there was any appreciable difference between orthodoxy and schism, should have the opportunity of seeing it.

In his father's time people had excused themselves in many plausible ways from going to church, because they saw no difference between the church and the chapel, other than that the chapel was the better warmed.

There are some very remarkable persons about,

about, who are always making speeches and
writing pamphlets against what they call
" giving an undue prominence to forms
and ceremonies." These quiet people, if
they could get their way, or any part of it,
would have nothing seemly in the house
of God—nothing but Dutch carpet and
electro-plate—and they look on everything
as an excess which happens to be decent.

There were some such at St. Hilda's.
They were afraid Crispin Ken would be
having an organ. They were afraid he
would magnify the authority of the Church
too much ; and that too much would have
been reached had he declared it at all.
They were afraid he would be preaching
in his surplice. " It would be such a pity,"
they said, with their best sectarian mildness,
" to contend for these little things when
they might very well offend so many."

It was very clear to Crispin Ken, that he
could only hope to fill the church, by showing that he had some authority for asking
people to come. His father had conceded
everything—all those "little things"—and

o 3   when

when he came to die, had nothing he could point to as gain. Those who had been lost by concession, could only be regained by showing, that there was more than had seemed between the church, and the meeting-house.

A man is written down an enthusiast and a fanatic, who thinks anything of the decencies of public worship ; and Crispin Ken was quite prepared to be told that he was unsettling the peace of the parish, and unnecessarily disquieting quiet people, if he insisted on these "little things." If there was to be the worship of the church at all, his people should know on what foundation the church stood. If there were to be any psalms or hymns, they should not be put up in a manner very bad to hear ; and if he was to wear anything about him when he preached, over and above his coat, it should at least be that for which there was authority.

The " Evangelical Protestant " thinks it a great pity to startle some people over that which is white, instead of over that which

is

is black. It only matters that the white is right, and that the black is wrong. There is nothing very new, in its very generally happening, that the wrong is nicest. Sympathy is always with those who want the wrong thing. The "advanced Evangelical Protestant" has at last come to ask, "Why wear anything at all?" "It may offend some consciences; your coat does very well." "Why have priests or deacons?—there are religious bankers." "Why have churches?—there are saloons and theatres. If you cannot get the lost into God's houses, you must get them in their own saloons to dance no more, and then begin to pray."

Crispin Ken meant to do what he should subscribe to, and he meant to do it all without an apology for being faithful. But he did not care to take the curacy from Mr. Lyle. Mr. Lyle had not asked him to take it; but Crispin knew that something had passed about it between his father and Mr. Lyle.

Every one he met had something to say

for

for Mr. Lyle. This man's little paraded power over all was becoming intolerable to Crispin. He had felt the influence that was so widely recognized himself, and Crispin could not get over it, that this power had once mastered him, even for so short a while.

He would have liked to have had words with Mr. Lyle; but Mr. Lyle was not the man to give him the occasion.

Crispin, look at it as he might, could not set aside the conviction, that Mr. Lyle was not what he seemed. That he was not nearly so good as the world believed him — but then he never seemed to be ought else. Never! and the worst amongst us cannot *always* act. It is hard to keep the counterfeit always in disguise.

There was nothing in the man that even ever touched suspicion. He was an influence in the Parliament of England. He was an influence on the platform that is inspired by Exeter Hall; but it was an influence that the middle men about him could not reach.

Crispin

Crispin Ken had watched him for a
week, had watched—wanting to find out
the counterfeit—and at the end he could
not find a cause for thinking the worse of
Ruy Lyle.

"I do not think I am wrong," said Crispin to himself, "I do not think this man
is what he seems." And whilst there was
so much to set suspicion down, there was
nothing that could give it any cause to
stay—nothing but that he seemed better
than a man can be—nothing *but that he
never looked you in the face.*

Since the death of Reuben Ken, those
at the curacy had lived on the few pounds
due to the curate at his death. Crispin
had proposed taking orders at the Easter
ordination. After that he did not know
what he should do ; Jack could live with
him, and perhaps it would be for the best
that Mona and Wycherley should be
married as soon as might be—as soon as
Wycherley was well again.

It was the same afternoon, that Crispin
had surprised himself in that Saturday re-

view,

view, that he made up his mind to speak to Mona, and abide by her decision, that there was certainly no ground just then for thinking ill of Mr. Lyle. In all that week Mr. Lyle had never let it seem that he was over Mona as her guardian. He insisted upon nothing. He did not force himself into her presence. Since the reading of the will, and since he had told her how he was her guardian, his authority had never been intruded. Mona even thought sometimes he was away too much. She had done everything she liked to do, but then, certainly, she had done nothing that he did not like.

Mona could not conceal from her own heart that his influence had been at work; and it was an influence that had grown up, so that it took a part in all she did. She had not seen him for a week, and yet she seemed to see him everywhere.

Crispin found his sister sitting buried with these thoughts when he came into the room. Mona started up and checked what was almost a scream.

" I

" I did not know it was you, Crispin, I thought it was—"

" You thought it was Mr. Lyle, Mona."

" How did you know that, Crispin ?"

" You are always thinking of that man, Mona."

" I am not always thinking of Mr. Lyle, Crispin; but I confess that his influence—"

" Influence, Mona — I am getting tired of this nonsense ; what is he but like another man ? He—"

" Did you ever see another that was like him, Crispin ?"

" When I tell you, that I often feel his influence and cannot throw it off, I can hardly tell you, Crispin, what I mean ; but did it never seem to you that he was speaking very near, that this Mr. Lyle *was* near, that you could even see his face, when it might be he was miles away ? "

Crispin *had* felt this, but he had fought against confessing it, so he did not answer what his sister said.

" Mona, you love this man, and there is that which tells me he has something to keep

keep back from the world — that he is not what he seems."

"Crispin, I could not love him if I would — I would not if I could ; but what do you mean by what you say ?"

"I only mean this, Mona, that I think that Ruy Lyle has done, I don't know when, some cursed thing ; he cannot be what he would seem. I have watched him as I never watched a man before ; but he always seems the same ; he gave no cause for me to at all suspect him."

"Then, Crispin, why be so suspicious ?"

"Ah, Mona, that is what the world would ask ; now, I cannot tell, but never will I rest until I can ; if he offers me this living, I do not think that I will take it."

"I think you will do wrong."

"You say so, Mona, because you cannot throw away his influence as I can ; but if I take it, it must be without condition."

"Don't talk so loud, Crispin, I'm sure he's coming."

"Did you hear him, Mona ?"

"No,

" No, I did not hear him."

" Has he told you he will come ? "

" I have not seen him for a week."

" Mona, this is worse than folly; you know that he is coming, yet you cannot hear or see him, and he has not told you that he is coming—but I think I hear his step."

There was no step; but ten minutes later Mr. Lyle entered the room. He always came when he was wanted.

" About this living, Mr. Ken ?"

Mona looked at Crispin, and the look meant, " he has heard all we have said, and yet he was not near."

" I promised your good father the day he died that it should be yours."

" I will take it," said Crispin to himself; " Mona will marry Wycherley when he is better, and then there cannot be much harm." And Crispin took it. It was offered too without condition.

" I don't think he can have done anything so very bad," said Mona, when Mr. Lyle had gone.

" You

" You could not love him, Mona, I believe ; but if you could, you would, I fear,"
was all that Crispin answered.

Crispin was ordained at Easter, got a
title from Mr. Wycherley, and was presented by Mr. Lyle with the perpetual
curacy of St. Hilda's the great.

Meanwhile it was quite impossible to
have words with Mr. Lyle. He never
seemed to come too often, and yet perhaps
Mona was a good deal at the Hall — more
than she confessed to.

John Wycherley was sometimes worse,
sometimes better ; never well enough for
his marriage with Mona to be fixed.

Crispin had a great deal to do, and a
great deal to contend against. The ene-
mies of the Church in those two-and-twenty
years had gathered strength. But he set
the Church before them, so that they might
see there *was* a Church, and that authority
and schism were not one.

Mr. Lyle, although known to be of a very
different way of thinking, did not interfere ;
and before many months were over, Crispin
had

had not only a better filled church, but tolerably well filled schools.

There was something too for the parish to read. Some objected to the psalms being sung, but there was no more need to listen than had they thought the sermon should not be said. They objected to as many things as would fill a chapter, and it is quite sufficiently well known what such object to. They did not think it well that Crispin should preach in white ; he might have, to please some, really preached in nothing.

Mr. Lyle had nothing to say ; but when Crispin put the better papers on the table in the library, and took the *Saturday Review*, Mr. Lyle called on Crispin Ken.

"You have taken the *Saturday Review*, Mr. Ken ; you have well considered what you are doing?"

"I have very well thought what I am doing, Mr. Lyle. I do not think with that paper on everything, but it has spoken out against that disguised schism, and that uncharitable ignorance of which Exeter Hall

Hall is the church and the *Record* the organ."

Crispin Ken, when he spoke, forgot that he was speaking to the greatest man " Evangelical " Protestantism ever had, or ever had bowed down to. But Mr. Lyle, if he felt it, did not seem to feel it; and if he did hate the paper, as it is its greatest praise to say his party always do, he did not seem to hate it. Crispin Ken had some cause to know that that man never showed what was within him.

" Miss Ken is to be married in the summer ?" How did he know this ? it had only been talked of that morning for the first time.

" Indeed, Mr. Lyle, I cannot tell how you should how it, for we only spoke of it this morning."

Crispin had meant by this that very likely Mr. Lyle was listening.

Mr. Lyle saw what was meant, but assuming to know that of which he had only heard something, he put it to Crispin as that which he had learnt.

" And

"And do you think that Mr. Wycherley will be ever well again?"

"Why not?" asked Crispin, "why do you ask that?" and he started up, he did not well know why.

"Because he is sometimes worse and sometimes better, Mr. Ken, but oftenest worse. Good morning—You might never have thought to watch that woman, I suppose?"

"Watch who? What woman?"

But Mr. Lyle was gone.

The words that he had dropped were working then, and afresh did Crispin seem to hear them. "Sometimes better, sometimes worse, but oftenest worse;" and he saw it all as he had never looked on it before. The man he tried to hate had spoken the word that might yet save Wycherley; that man had quickened in his mind a hideous thought. He buried his face in his hands to hide it out, but it seemed like a spectre sitting there; and he hurried on and never stayed till he had reached John Wycherley; and John Wycherley was just

drinking

drinking from a cup held to his lips by Meg. The devilry he dared not think of was before him ; and everywhere did Crispin seem to see a face, and in each face the cold calm mocking smile of Ruy Lyle.

End of the First Volume.

LONDON
PRINTED BY SPOTTISWOODE AND CO.
NEW-STREET SQUARE.

By the fame Author,

MIRIAM MAY.

THE TWELFTH THOUSAND.

Opinions of the Prefs on " Miriam May."

THE STANDARD.

This is not one of thofe novels which will die in a few weeks. We fhall not anticipate the pleafure our readers will derive from its perufal by attempting any fketch of the plot. But we may fay that the life of Miriam May, from the workhoufe door to the Court of St. James's, is a moft interefting, natural, and well-told romance. It is, what it purports to be, a ftory of real life. The writing is unaffected, pleafing, and powerful. It is a fiction every one fhould read; and it is a fiction, we underftand, that all the world is reading. Our political friends will find the hypocrify of Liberalifm in electioneering admirably fhown up; and the Bifhop-making of the Whigs is not the lefs ably but truthfully expofed.

THE CRITIC.

" Miriam May " is a real romance, and it is well done.

JOHN BULL.

Before we have been enabled to notice the firft edition of this work, fo great has been the demand for it that it has already reached a third edition. This is not to be attributed fimply to it being a fingle-volume novel, though that is in itfelf a great advantage, but is mainly owing to its being at once interefting as a ftory, while at the fame time it is really a firft-rate political novel. We will not fpoil our reader's intereft in the work by following the heroine's varying fortunes, but will briefly point out fome of its excellences as a political narrative. The object of the book is at once to expofe, which it does moft completely, how thoroughly Liberalifm is a fham, and how the higheft offices in the Church are bartered by the Whigs. The letter of Lord Kantwell to the Hon. and Rev. Calvin Slie — the originals of which our readers will at once recognife — is one of the beft things we have met with for a long time. One of the incidents, viz., the praying for anything but a blefling on the labours of a brother clergyman, we fhould have confidered a grofs exaggeration, did we not unhappily know that juft fuch an occurrence took place in the Weft End of this metropolis, the principal actor being one of the Palmerftonian Bifhops. The reader's intereft throughout is thoroughly fuftained, and many will not clofe the book till they have finifhed it. Altogether we pronounce it a firft-rate novel, and heartily wifh it every fuccefs.

LITERARY GAZETTE.

Bitternefs is of various kinds as well as various degrees. There is the mellow bitternefs of the hop, there is the pungent bitternefs of a Seville orange, there is the four bitternefs of quaffia or of gentian ; there is the bitternefs of cynicifm, of hatred, of difappointment ; and there is perhaps a more reputable bitternefs, having its root in a keen difcrimination and intenfe difapproval of falfehood and wrong-doing. The volume before us is of this laft defcription. Its acrimony is indeed acrimony, but it does not feem to fpring from any felfifh mifanthropy or morbid difappointment. It is rather the overflowing of hot indignation againft malignity under the cloak of charity. We confefs we have fcarcely ever come cross a work containing so much concentrated invective, or such relentless tearing away of the veils which society allows to conceal insincerity and malice. However, we believe, from the tone of "Miriam May," that its author has been animated by no other motive than a desire to lash, with merited severity, religious hypocrisy, and to administer a deserved rebuke to uncharitableness and malice. As such, we consider its remarkable popularity a most healthy sign of the times — a popularity too which must infallibly tend to throw into confusion the class of persons whom its pages so fiercely denounce, and whose practices they so relentlessly expose.

In conclusion, we consider this novel very remarkable both for the keen way in which it sees through hypocrisy and roguery, and for the vigorous force with which it chastises impostors. Though perhaps occasionally a little too bitter in its tone, it is still a faithful exposure of evil, and as such we welcome it.

Weekly Mail.

"Miriam May" is a more than ordinary good novel; and, being so, has in a few months gained a very enviable—and certainly a very deservable — measure of popularity. When we add that everything is wrought with constructive skill and technical ability, we are quite sure we have said enough to set our novel-loving readers craving for the book. It is but fair to them, however, and to the author, to add that "Miriam May" is not merely a novel. There are many pages in it devoted to a judicious and judicial consideration of the cardinal topics — religious, political, and social — of the hour; and our author, without greatly interfering with the course of his narrative, manages to give us, in pithy and pleasant manner, many new and profound notions on a variety of subjects. Altogether, we have not met with a book for many a long day which has given us so much satisfaction: and the very merits of the work itself suggest a canon of criticism which we should not think of applying to one novel out of a thousand.

The Atlas.

Disappointed people declare that "luck's everything;" but, if we examine a "success," we shall find it was achieved by those qualities which deserved it. The work before us has reached a fourth edition, and no one, except an unsuccessful novelist, can read it without admitting that the popularity is deserved. The story is well constructed, and the characters are elaborately and faithfully delineated. We regard it as a good sign of the times that "Miriam May" has had, and still has, a large circulation. It contains some things that may offend our prejudices; from some of its conclusions we may conscientiously dissent; but there is much in it with which we must agree, and which is calculated to advance the interests of religion by exposing the folly and wickedness of canting professions.

Dispatch.

"Miriam May" is the title of a very charming story. The heroism of the mother — who for some twenty odd years submits to the insolent sneers of a small township, with its equivalent amount of tea and scandal, highly fashionable, and crammed to the teeth with "respectability," during which time she has been a wife and wedded mother, the ring being put aside for purposes the story itself explains — is of the noblest order. Descriptively, the fiction is excellent.

Plymouth Mail.

"Miriam May," a one-volume novel, only just published, is yet in its fourth edition. The earnestness of the writer — his energetic style often rising to eloquence — his cordial sympathies, and equally cordial antipathies — render the book a most absorbing one. The Hon. and Rev. Calvin Slie, who is made a Bishop when Lord Fripton is Premier, is a capital satirical sketch.